New York Times bestselling author Donna Alward returns to Harlequin Romance with a brand-new duet!

Marrying a Millionaire

These tycoons make a match in a million!

Best friends wedding planner Adele and photographer Harper are in the business of happily-ever-afters, yet haven't found their own!

The arrival of two brothers, tycoons Dan and Drew, in their Banff winter wonderland may be about to change all that...

Could two Rocky Mountain marriages—and a pregnancy twist!—be in the cards?

Find out in

Best Man for the Wedding Planner

Available now!

And don't miss

Secret Millionaire for the Surrogate

Coming January 2019!

Dear Reader,

It's true that each book an author writes has something of themselves in it. How could it not? We bring our beliefs and our values and life experiences to our characters. But sometimes what we bring is even more tangible...in the form of an "it happened to me" scene.

There's one of those scenes in this book...during Adele and Dan's ski trip. The circumstances surrounding Adele's not-so-graceful tumble are straight from life experience. Granted, I was at Panorama Mountain Resort and not Sunshine in Banff, but when you read that section, realize that it's pretty much exactly how it happened to me...though I'm convinced I ended up with a light concussion. I keep saying that with a bottom the size of mine, it makes no sense that my center of gravity seems to be my head, but there you go.

It was such a pleasure to write this book and be back with the Harlequin Romance line again. I hope you'll come back next month for Harper and Drew's story.

My very best wishes,

Donna

Best Man for the Wedding Planner

Donna Alward

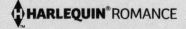
HARLEQUIN®ROMANCE

Recycling programs
for this product may
not exist in your area.

ISBN-13: 978-1-335-13541-4

Best Man for the Wedding Planner

First North American publication 2018

Printed in U.S.A.

Donna Alward lives on Canada's east coast with her family, which includes her husband, a couple of kids, a senior dog and two crazy cats. Her heartwarming stories of love, hope and homecoming have been translated into several languages, hit bestseller lists and won awards, but her favorite thing is hearing from readers! When she's not writing she enjoys reading (of course!), knitting, gardening, cooking... and is a *Masterpiece Theatre* addict. You can visit her on the web at donnaalward.com and join her mailing list at donnaalward.com/newsletter.

Visit the Author Profile page
at Harlequin.com for more titles.

To Carly and Sheila and the UK office...
It's good to be home.

Praise for
Donna Alward

"This is Donna Alward at her best.... Her stories
are homey and comfy and gentle—this one is no
different."

CHAPTER ONE

IF THE BRIDE changed her mind about something one more time, Adele was going to lose it. And she didn't often feel that way. Brides who got jitters or last-minute second thoughts about their ceremony were commonplace enough. But this bride...

She was sweet and lovely, but such a micromanager that Adele was ready to tell her to go to the spa for the next forty-eight hours and not come back until she was as buffed and polished as the ice sculptures due to be delivered just after the wedding but before the reception.

"Are you sure the calla lilies are the right flowers for the centerpieces?" Holly asked, worrying her lip with her French-tipped nail.

"Yes," Adele replied decisively. "They're elegant and perfect for the arrangements you picked." She inhaled calmly and put a reassuring hand on the bride's arm. "Trust me on this. Your wedding is going to be perfect. Every detail is sorted, and in two days you're going to stand here in the great hall and get married and it's going to be magical."

She looked around at the majestic hall of the famed Fiori Cascade Hotel and gave a little wistful sigh. It wasn't her first wedding here, but each time she put one together she did a little daydreaming of her own. Sometimes the great hall was the setting; other times it was a smaller, more intimate room. In the summer, weddings on the stone patio with the Rockies forming a dramatic backdrop stole her breath. They were fairy tales, every last one of them.

But fairy tales were for other women. Not for her. Instead she put her heart and soul into creating a perfect day for each deserving couple. It was incredibly rewarding and affirming even if, on days like today, her patience was tested.

"Are you sure? Maybe we should have had roses, or gardenia or something?" Holly asked.

"I'm positive." She smiled and pulled out her tablet. "And everything is right on schedule. Tomorrow we have the rehearsal and the

dinner afterward. The menu is set and the
wine selections made. All your wedding party
has to do is show up." She gave a little laugh,
trying to dispel the bride's nerves. "Holly,
you're having your wedding in one of the
most beautiful hotels in the world. Trust the
staff to do their jobs, and let me look after
the details, so you can enjoy your big day."

A little voice in her head added, *and the
lifetime to follow*, but she didn't say the words
out loud. She was a wedding planner, not a
marriage counselor. Once the last glass of
champagne was drunk, her job was over.
Each time she finished a job, she sent the
bride and groom off with a hope for happiness in the future. The wedding was only one
day, but marriage was for a lifetime. Or at
least, it was supposed to be.

Holly smiled. "Okay." Then she let out a
big breath. "Okay," she repeated, laughing a
little. "I swear, Adele, I didn't mean to become a bridezilla."

Adele smiled warmly as her irritation evaporated. "You're used to being the one looking after the details. I get it. But your job is
to delegate and trust that we know what we're
doing. And we do," she added. "I promise."

In five years of planning weddings, there

hadn't been a situation she couldn't handle or remedy, most times without the bride and groom or the guests even guessing that anything had gone awry. Crisis management was something she was good at, and the time crunch of the wedding day barely ruffled her feathers.

"The wedding party arrives today, and we're going out for some fun tonight," Holly said, her posture much more relaxed as they walked to the door of the massive ballroom. "I think I might need it."

"No bachelor party or bachelorette?"

Holly shook her head. "We decided against it. Pete's best man is coming in from Toronto, and my maid of honor is pregnant, and the rest of the wedding party is all from Calgary and we went out a while ago." A blush colored her cheeks, and Adele wondered why. A crazy hen night, perhaps? "Anyway, we're just going to head into town for some dinner and maybe a few drinks. Keep it low-key."

Considering the wedding was definitely not low-key, Adele was surprised. But low-key in Banff could still be pricey, and Pete and Holly weren't sparing any expense. It was one of the most lavish weddings Adele had ever planned.

"Sounds lovely," she replied as they stopped just inside the door. Adele reached for her coat; tomorrow and the next day would be incredibly long and right now she wanted to head home, respond to some emails and phone calls from her in-house office, and then have a glass of wine and some dinner and fall into bed.

She shrugged into her heavy coat and reached inside the pocket for gloves. At least the happy couple had decided on a January wedding and Holly wasn't being married at Christmas. That might have been a little too hokey. Holly had indeed wanted red as her color at first, but Adele had shown her some photos of other weddings and convinced her to go with navy and silver. Far less predictable, especially now that the holiday decorations were down. Instead of red and green, they could use the cool blues to focus on snowflakes and winter.

"Oh!" Holly stopped and turned back. "I meant to ask you about the ice sculptures. Is there any way we can make them last longer? It would be so neat to have them last all the way through the evening."

The sculptures weren't huge and unless they were put outside, they would melt at a pace consistent with the temperature of the room. "We'll put them out at the last possible minute," Adele assured her. "But it depends on the heat of the room. That's one thing I can't control," she advised, and put her handbag over her shoulder. "It's a huge room, but the temp goes up when it's filled with people."

Holly looked disappointed, but didn't persist, much to Adele's relief. They were just making their way to the lobby when Holly gave a squeal and picked up her pace.

"Lisa! Dan!"

Adele was adjusting her purse strap, but when she finally looked up, her heart froze and her feet stopped moving. Holly skipped forward and hugged first the woman, and then the man standing in a tan wool coat with one hand on the handle of his suitcase and a garment bag over his other arm.

Dan. Just saying his name in her head made her heart squeeze a little. Daniel Brimicombe. Of all the Dans in Toronto, *he* had to be the best man. It was too far-fetched to be even comical, but here he was, in the flesh, smiling widely for the bride. The man Adele had once planned to marry. The one who'd whispered plans in her ear in the dark.

The man whose heart she'd broken…and in the breaking of it, broke her own.

Best man Dan.

Adele Hawthorne, wedding planner extraordinaire, solver of problems and manager of crises, stood rooted to the spot with her mouth dropped open and her hands hanging uselessly at her sides. This was one wrinkle that she hadn't seen coming.

"Did you come from the airport together? How smart! Come on, meet my wedding planner. She's amazing."

Adele heard the words and tried to unscramble the mess that was her brain. Dan hadn't noticed her yet, thankfully. She was still trying to recover, and it was difficult because he hadn't changed at all. Oh, sure, there was a slight maturity in his face but really… it was like it had been eight days rather than eight years since they'd seen each other. Dark, perfect hair, just a little stubble on his chin, and the way his coat fit on his shoulders…as if it had been specifically tailored for his build.

He'd always carried himself with that calm confidence. She'd envied it back then. Still did.

And then he adjusted his garment bag, turned around and saw her.

His face paled. "Delly?"

Her throat tightened. Damn. He'd used his old nickname for her, and that made it a hundred times worse. She wasn't Delly. Not anymore.

"You know Adele? Oh, my God, that's so weird!" Holly seemed totally unaware of the shock rippling between Adele and Dan, though Lisa—whom Adele knew was one of the bridesmaids—seemed to be cluing in.

Dan recovered first, and the color came back in his cheeks as he smiled. The smile didn't quite reach his eyes. "We knew each other in university. I haven't seen her in eight years."

Eight years, seven months and a couple of weeks, if they were going to be exact about it. "Hi, Dan. It's good to see you." It wasn't a lie. It was a huge mess, but it was good to see him. What had happened hadn't been his fault. He'd done nothing wrong.

His eyes widened as if he couldn't believe she'd said such a thing, and then he nodded. "Likewise."

Holly finally sensed the tension and stepped in, looking back and forth at them with a small wrinkle between her eyebrows. "You should see the job she's done putting all this together. I would have been so lost." She smiled, but it had a worried edge to it.

Lisa held out her hand. "Hi, I'm one of the bridesmaids. Did you help find the dresses? Because I love mine."

"Oh, I'm glad," Adele answered, smiling through her anxiety. "There'll be a seamstress here tomorrow for any last-minute alterations." She chanced a look at Dan. "For the groomsmen, too. In case anything needs adjusting."

"Great."

The rock in the pit of her stomach got heavier.

"Listen," Holly said, "why don't you two catch up? Dan, we're having dinner in town tonight. I'm sure Pete's given you the details."

"Actually, he hasn't, and I'd like to get settled and make a few phone calls before we go out. There are a few things I forgot to tell my assistant before I left."

Assistant. She didn't even know what he'd done after he'd finished his business degree.

Plus, he'd basically just said that he had no interest in talking to her at all. Not that she deserved any consideration. She'd never told him the real reason why she'd broken off their relationship, only that she didn't feel the same anymore. It had been a lie, but at the time she felt it was the kindest thing to say.

As the trio walked away toward the elevators, Adele swallowed the lump in her throat. It hadn't been a complete lie, after all. She hadn't felt the same after she'd left her doctor's office. Her feelings for Dan hadn't changed, but her feelings about herself and her place in his life had.

The word *cancer* tended to do that. Especially paired with the word *infertility*. She'd known he'd be better off without her.

Dan had to stop gritting his teeth so tightly. If he didn't, he was going to give himself a toothache, a headache or both.

But seeing Adele this afternoon had been so unexpected that he hadn't had any time to think or prepare. It had just hit him—*wham*—right in the solar plexus.

"Another beer, Dan?" Pete nudged his arm.

He shrugged. "Why not?"

Pete ordered another round as the noise in the pub got louder. Was he getting old? At first Pete's younger sister had suggested a nightclub, but the idea of a crowded place with too much bass and bodies grinding was unappealing. Dan had assumed tonight would be a little more upscale, but instead they'd hit one of the local pubs. He was glad of it, actually—it had been too long since he'd chilled out in such a relaxed atmosphere.

He looked over at Pete and gave a grin. "This reminds me of when we both started with the company. Paying off student loans and heading for wherever had cheap beer and a decent steak sandwich."

Pete lifted his glass. "Those were the days, huh? Just like old times."

Yeah, it was. Sometimes he missed it. Now he put in longer days and drinks and dinner were usually business events and not downtime.

He sat back in his chair and let out a sigh. He'd had a good steak and some cold beer and was looking forward to being back in his room and in a comfortable bed. It was past ten, which meant it was past midnight home in Toronto, and he wasn't in a party mood. He was finally taking a whole week's vacation and *she* had to be here. Seeing Adele had taken his celebratory mood and soured it, despite the *old times* feel to the evening.

The waitress came back with a tray of drinks and put one down in front of him, offering a bright smile. He smiled back, but only out of politeness. She was pretty enough, but once again Adele was in the front of his thoughts. He resented her being there. He'd moved on with his life. She hadn't really given him a choice about that.

"Dude, are you all right? You look ready to kill someone." Pete took a drink of his own beer and lifted an eyebrow.

"Didn't Holly tell you?"

"Tell me what?"

He took a long drink of the brew and put the glass down on the table. "Your wedding planner is my ex."

"Denise?"

Dan shook his head. "No, of course not. I was never serious about her. I mean *the* ex."

The emphasis was all that was needed. "Oh. The one from university."

"Yeah. And I had no idea. Just boom. There she was, standing in the lobby this afternoon."

"How does she look?"

He picked up his beer again and angled an eyebrow. "You've met her."

Pete laughed. "I mean, how does she look to you?"

His brain conjured up an image of her standing in the lobby, her warm coat bundled around her, her eyes wide and startled to see him, too. "Too good," he admitted, and finished the glass. The drinks were going down a little too easily, but there was a limo waiting for all of them to take them back to the hotel. He only had to stagger from the car to his room. Then maybe he'd fall asleep and forget about her.

Pete nodded. "I'm sorry, man. We had no idea."

"How could you? It's halfway across the country." He and Pete had been fresh out of university, and met working for the same eco-energy company in Toronto. Pete's career had taken him to Alberta, the oil-and-gas capital of Canada, while Dan had stayed in Toronto, rising up through the ranks until he was chief financial officer of the company. It was a massive achievement to reach that level before he was thirty.

"What are you going to do about it?"

Dan looked up at Pete, realizing that despite the generous slab of beef and fries he'd eaten, his reflexes were slowing. No more beer for him. "Nothing. It's your wedding, and she's supposed to be making it amazing. I'll just avoid her is all. Shouldn't be too hard." After all, he'd been avoiding thinking about her for at least the last eight years. It had taken nearly two of those years for him to even start dating again. Not that he'd admit that out loud.

Pete grinned. "Well, Lisa's been looking at you all night. And I know she's single. Might be a good distraction for you."

Dan considered. The blonde was cute, for sure, with an easy smile and an attractive figure, particularly in the leggings and snug sweater she'd worn tonight. But he shook his head. "I don't think so, pal. Wedding hook-ups can be messy, and I'm not in the mood to play games."

Even if, by doing so, he could give Adele a glimpse of what she'd walked away from.

He didn't want revenge. He just wanted to put her in his rearview mirror for good.

The subject was dropped for a while, and after one more round of drinks the group departed for the limo and the hotel. Tomorrow they had free time until the rehearsal at six, with the exception of the last-minute fittings.

As he opened the door to his room, he realized he was looking forward to a morning of actually sleeping in and maybe going for a hike or something. He hadn't been to Banff since he was in high school on a class trip to

Calgary. The only thing that would make it better was if his brother, Drew, was here. His younger brother lived for the outdoors, and the wilder, the better. The opulence of the hotel was great, but right now Dan missed his family. They were all grown and spread out all over the country. Drew wasn't even in Canada all that often anymore. When had they become so divided?

The bed was turned down and he crawled inside, the ache in his gut growing hollower by the minute. Family…love…it seemed both had taken a back seat to success. Or maybe it was that he'd tried to use success to fill the absence of close relationships in his life. Even the women he'd dated…he didn't ever get too close to them. Why?

He flopped to his side and sighed. And maybe he should stop thinking so much. Damn Adele for being here, and for dredging up all these feelings, anyway.

The wedding was the day after tomorrow. She was the planner. After that, he wouldn't need to see her at all, would he?

And he could enjoy what remained of his vacation and go back to his regularly scheduled life.

Without her.

CHAPTER TWO

A WAITRESS REFILLED Adele's coffee without asking as Adele opened her spreadsheet with today's itemized list. The hotel coffee shop had become her temporary office, as it allowed her to be closer to everyone involved than her home office did.

Still, her stomach was in knots, and it was more to do with seeing Dan than the wedding. The distraction was stealing her focus. By tomorrow, changes couldn't be made. Everything had to be in place by tonight.

Her email notification dinged quietly and she let out a frustrated sigh. Holly and Pete had been talking about the cocktail hour and wanted a change made to the signature drink and an addition to the hors d'oeuvre menu. Two extra people were now attending who had declined before, so final plate numbers also needed to be adjusted. And they were family, so the seating arrangements would have to be tweaked, too.

Nothing was earth-shattering, but Adele seriously appreciated those brides who knew what they wanted, set it up and stayed the course. Still, the fee from this event was significant, and as long as everything went off without a hitch, it was a great addition to her portfolio. She was smart enough to know a lot of her grumpiness was brought on from the arrival of Dan. Particularly since he'd plainly shunned her yesterday.

She took a sip of coffee, her stomach rumbled, and she knew she had to eat some breakfast before tackling anything. Within moments, she'd ordered an apple Danish and yogurt—something healthy to balance out the sweet pastry. Dutifully, she ate the yogurt first, and had just taken a first sticky bite of Danish when Dan walked in, dressed in jeans and a sweater so cozy and soft that he looked incredibly huggable. Add to that his thick, dark hair and the shadow of stubble on his jaw and hers wasn't the only head that turned.

He saw her sitting there and his jaw tightened, his initial relaxed expression evaporating. The nerves that had already been dancing in her stomach started a jig and she put the pastry back on the plate. The fact that he still seemed to despise her put her on edge, but not as much as her own reaction. Today, like yesterday, there'd been a split second of happiness and warmth when she'd looked up and seen him there. As if her heart reacted before her brain could kick in and say, "No, Delly. He's not for you anymore." The truth was, it still hurt.

He hesitated, but then came over. "I didn't expect to see you here," he said quietly, standing beside her table.

"It's the easiest place to have a base of operations the day before the wedding," she replied, trying a smile. "Do you want to join me? You look like you could use your first morning coffee."

There was a slight pause, and then he said, "Why not?" and pulled out the chair opposite her.

Adele wiped her sticky fingers on her napkin. "The baked goods here are to die for. Though they do have some breakfast sandwich options, so you can have your eggs."

The look on his face was so startled that she blushed. "I mean, if you still like eggs for breakfast. Not that I'd know. Just that you used to…" The heat in her cheeks deepened. "I'm sorry. This is awkward."

"You think?" he said, but then smiled a little, dispelling a tiny bit of the tension. "Actually, it makes me feel better knowing you feel awkward. Yesterday you were so…together."

"I wasn't, really," she admitted. She met his gaze. "To be honest, seeing you was a huge shock. I honestly didn't know you were in the wedding."

"How could you?" He shrugged, and then ordered coffee and "anything with bacon in it" to eat. When the waitress left again, he rested his elbows on the table. "I suppose talking this morning should help clear the air. Then we can go through the wedding without any weird vibes."

It sounded very logical and smart, except there were already vibes. Adele had walked away eight years ago, but not because she had stopped loving him. In a way, it was because she'd cared about him so much. As her Aunt Sally would say, sometimes you had to let a bird go. And if it came back to you, it was meant to be. Dan hadn't come back. And she'd built herself a good life in the intervening years.

Still, seeing him brought back way too many memories and feelings.

His breakfast arrived and Adele made a point of taking another big drink of coffee as he added milk to his cup. The shop was quiet; this was not the hotel's busiest season, though there were always groups of skiers who, at this hour, were probably already on the slopes.

He put down his spoon and met her gaze again. "So, a wedding planner. How long have you been doing this?"

She cupped her hands around her mug. "Oh, five years now? On my own, at least. I started working for a company in Vancouver, and then I came to Banff with a coworker one summer to help with an event. I fell in love with the area, relocated and started my own business."

"Risky."

She nodded. "It was. But I started small, and now I run it from my home. The office space is downstairs, on the main floor, and the upstairs is my living area." She relaxed a little, pleased that they could manage small talk. "How about you? You're still in Toronto?"

He nodded. "I'm CFO of a clean energy company now. I actually took next week off so I could enjoy a bit of a vacation here. Then I'll stop in at the new Calgary office for a day or so before I head back. It's been a small operation for the last two years, but we're putting things in motion to make it our western hub."

"Wow. That's...great. And you sound as if you love it."

"Yep."

She tried a small smile. "I guess we turned out okay then, haven't we?"

He didn't answer, just reached for his sandwich. As he lifted it, she noticed there was no ring on his left hand. "Not married, then," she said quietly.

"Nope. No girlfriend, either. Though that's a new development."

"I'm sorry."

He shrugged. "Don't be. It had run its course."

He sounded so casual, so blasé about it. Adele sat back in her chair and frowned a little. Small talk was well and good, but there was still a wall between them. Perhaps there always would be. It was a wall she'd built, so she could hardly complain about it, could she?

"And your family? They're well?"

That, at least, prompted a genuine smile.

"They are. Mom and Dad still live in Barrie and we kids are spread all over, but we get together a few times a year and video chat. Morgan has twin babies now. Girls."

"You're an uncle."

He grinned and nodded. "They're three months old. And Tamara is expecting another boy. She and Chris already have two."

"Two! Your parents must be thrilled. I know how much they love having a big family."

She really did know. The "big family" had been a big reason why she'd walked away from Dan and the whole Brimicombe clan. Each time they'd visited, his parents had gone on and on about big families and grandkids and having a house full of babies. Dan had said on more than one occasion that being a Brimicombe meant being a part of a big, happy family. That he wanted at least three or four kids of his own, so that all the cousins and siblings could grow up together, as they had.

Finding out she could never give him the children he wanted had nearly destroyed her. She hadn't wanted him to be destroyed, too. Or for his family to pretend it didn't matter when it was so obvious it would.

"They're over the moon," he replied softly. "Four grandkids, another on the way and apparently we're just getting started. Dad wants enough to field his own softball team."

There was a tone in his voice she couldn't ignore. Was it that he wasn't contributing to the grandkid count? Or was it deeper than that? He'd wanted children and still didn't have any. Even though there was lots of time—he wouldn't be thirty for another four months—she wondered if seeing his sisters with babies was highlighting something he was missing.

"What about Drew?" she asked, changing the subject to the baby of the family. "What's he up to these days?"

Dan laughed. "Drew never stays in one place for long. He's busy setting up Aspen Outfitters locations all around North America. But he gets home a lot to visit. Dad's sixtieth is coming up in a few months. I know he's planning to be home for that." Dan laughed. "Somehow he always manages to drag me out in the wilderness with him for a few days. He tells me if I don't do that more often, I'll have to have my phone surgically removed."

"Sounds about right." She took another bite of Danish, chewed, swallowed and tried not to feel self-conscious. "I will say, despite it being very touristy around here, unplugging and going for a walk in the mountains does a lot for stress levels."

"I can see that. I'd forgotten how stunning it is. I'm hoping to do some skiing while I'm here. Get out and breathe the mountain air."

Quiet settled around them. Did they have nothing more to say to each other? She self-consciously ran a hand over her hair, which was still precisely anchored in her topknot. Adele thought about filling the quiet with the action of finishing her breakfast, but she wasn't hungry anymore. Her laptop screen had gone dark several minutes ago, so she tapped a key to bring it to life again.

"I'm holding you up from your work," Dan said, pushing back his chair.

"No, not really." She bit down on her lip. Hadn't she just touched the keys to fill the awkward gap? Now, at the first moment he moved to leave, she didn't want him to go. She was an idiot, plain and simple.

"It's okay. You don't have to be polite. I have a fitting in an hour, anyway." He patted his flat belly. "Gotta make sure the tuxedo fits."

He was going to be so dashing. She swallowed tightly, thinking about it. Seeing Dan wasn't just seeing an ex; it was coming face-to-face with the life she might have had if her illness hadn't stolen it all away. And yet seeing Dan's face as he talked about having nieces and nephews reassured her it had been the right thing. Dan deserved babies, and lots of them. He would have been supportive and said it didn't matter, but she knew it did. That it would eat away at him until their relationship paid the price.

And she hadn't been honest about why she was leaving because she'd been too afraid he'd be able to convince her to stay.

"If you have any questions, I'll be around the hotel all day." Adele smiled, though her heart wasn't quite in it. "Holly and Pete have some last-minute changes, and we're setting up for the rehearsal in the hall this afternoon."

He got up, took his wallet out of his back pocket and put a twenty down on the table. "I'm glad we talked, Delly," he said quietly. "This doesn't have to be weird. And after tomorrow, we won't see each other, anyway."

"Sure," she agreed, but a weight settled around her heart. It might not be weird for him, but it certainly was for her. She'd spent eight years convincing herself she'd done the right thing. Sometimes she questioned whether she should have kept the truth from him. But then she reminded herself that she'd set him free to be happy. She'd wanted that for Dan. Wanted him to have the family he'd always talked about.

But she had forgotten to take into account how much she'd loved him. And how hard it would be to ignore those old feelings if they came face-to-face again.

Dan walked into the rehearsal with his nerves already on edge. This morning's breakfast had taken his thoughts and turned them into a huge jumble of resentment and nostalgia. He'd spent a long time hating Adele for breaking his heart, but then he'd moved past it—at least mostly. Now and again he was reminded that he had an issue with trusting anyone, but as far as feelings for Adele…they'd faded.

Except they hadn't, really. Being here, with her, took all the feelings he'd thought he'd locked away for good and sent them bubbling to the surface. He'd loved her more than she could ever know. A man didn't get over that easily. Or, apparently, at all.

What were you supposed to do when The One wasn't really The One at all?

The rest of the wedding party milled about the hall, their voices echoing through the huge space. He shoved his hands in his pockets and looked around. Chairs were set up on either side of the aisle… Were they actually painted silver? He looked closer. They were. And each chair had a swath of fabric woven through the top rungs in rich navy. The effect was stunning.

The knot of people at the back of the aisle moved and revealed Adele, deftly weaving more fabric through the slats. She was still in the dark trousers and sweater that she'd worn this morning, but some of her hair had come loose from her knot. Had she been working all day? It was nearly seven and she had several chairs to finish.

She stood, put her hands on her lower back and stretched. The movement emphasized the curve of her breasts and the long column of her neck before she relaxed again and reached inside a box for another strip of material.

Everyone else simply milled about, oblivious to how Adele was still working while they chatted and laughed.

Holly saw him standing in the doorway and beckoned him over. "Come on in, Dan! Meet our officiant, Ms. Fraser. She'll be performing the ceremony tomorrow."

He was aware of Adele looking up, then back down again as he strode toward the assembled group. "Ms. Fraser," he said, shaking her hand. "I'm Dan Brimicombe, the best man."

"Pleased to meet you. And now that we're all here, we can get started." She laughed a little, a warm and friendly sound. "I know you all want to get this part over with so you can have dinner. I'll try to keep it painless."

Over the next half hour, Ms. Fraser deftly positioned everyone where they were supposed to be and ran through the order of the service. At one point she asked Adele a question about the placement of the musicians—a string quartet would be playing the processional and recessional—and then carried on. Dan looked over his shoulder and noticed she still had at least a dozen chairs or more to finish. He frowned. Wasn't this the job of the hotel staff? Surely she wasn't doing this all herself.

He stood at the front and waited as they ran through the processional yet again, the bridesmaids and bride coming up the aisle and moving into position. It gave him an unfettered view of Adele as she worked, tucking a stray strand of hair behind her ear, reaching into the box for more material as she made her way down the row. Someone from the hotel came in with a dolly and what appeared to be a dozen potted trees. As he half listened to the instructions about witnessing the marriage license, he watched Adele instruct the hotel employee and then help unload the ungainly pots and put them into position. As the employee wheeled the dolly back out again, he watched as Adele heaved a sigh, gave a stretch and then went back to work.

After thirty minutes, Ms. Fraser let everyone go except the bride and groom; she had a few final things to discuss with them before everyone departed for the onsite restaurant and the rehearsal dinner. He took the opportunity to go over to Adele. She had just finished tying a strip of satin to a chair and turned to fetch another piece when he held it up for her.

"Oh," she said, clearly startled. "Thank you, Dan."

"Have you done all these chairs yourself?"

She shrugged, anchored one end of the fabric and began weaving. "I had someone for the first thirty or so, but it was the end of her workday, and she wasn't feeling well. I sent her home."

"So you're doing it yourself."

"It's no big deal. I'd rather have her away from me if she has the flu or something. It's been going around."

He frowned. "Did you eat dinner yet?"

She laughed. "I'll eat when I get home later. The day before a wedding is always crazy. I'm used to this."

She finished off the chair, leaving a trail of navy satin that looked to be the exact same length as the other chairs. "How do you even do that?" he asked, impressed.

She took another piece of satin from his fingers. "If you always start in the same place, you end in the same place, too."

"I suppose you're right. Is this all you have to do tonight?"

She paused in her weaving and looked up at him. "No. All the trees that just came in? They all need white twinkly lights put on them."

"But there's…twelve."

"I know. I counted." She laughed then, a tired sound, but a happy one, too. "Seriously, Dan. This is not my first wedding. Look, everyone's getting ready to leave for the dinner. I've got this."

She threaded the fabric and tied it off again, moving down a chair.

"I just think it's a lot of work for one person. And it's Holly and Pete's wedding. They should—"

She stood up and faced him. "They should what?" she interrupted. "This is my job. This is what they pay me to do, and they're paying me quite well, so why don't you leave me to it instead of slowing me down?"

He stared at her, his lip curling as her irritated voice carried through the hall. A few people stopped and looked in their direction. Perfect. It was bad enough that Pete and Holly knew that Adele was his ex. Getting in an argument would only prompt more questions. If she wanted to do this all by herself, fine. He'd only been trying to help.

"I wouldn't want to stand in your way," he replied, a touch of acid in his words. "I guess I should have realized you like to be on your own, rather than a team player."

It was a cheap remark but one that he'd perhaps been holding inside for a long, long time. When they'd been together, they'd insisted that they were a team. A partnership. The abrupt change in their relationship had left him floundering. How did someone say she was your partner and then just move on without a backward glance?

This morning had been a mistake. He shouldn't have stopped for breakfast with her. He should have listened to his gut from the day before and stayed far, far away. Leave the past in the past.

He walked away before she had a chance to turn her back on him once again.

CHAPTER THREE

SHE COULDN'T GET WARM.

Adele hadn't been lying when she'd said the flu was going around, but she really hadn't considered the possibility of actually getting it. And not on the day of the biggest wedding of her career. She stepped under the hot spray of the shower, which felt glorious. She'd have to work through it, that was all. She'd stop at the pharmacy for meds, drink lots of fluids and power through. And wash her hands—a lot. She didn't feel great, but it wasn't anything she couldn't handle.

She dressed in a variation of her standard uniform, which was generally a little black dress that lent an air of professionalism while also allowing her to blend in with the guests. Today, however, the idea of black stockings and high heels and semi-bare arms was just... no. Instead she pulled out a soft pair of black trousers, her most comfortable heels and a black cashmere sweater. She'd be a little bit underdressed, but she'd be able to do her job and would blend into the background, as it should be. Tea, some acetaminophen, and she'd be right as rain.

She stopped at the drugstore and then for a smoothie, going for a massive vitamin injection. By the time she arrived at the hotel, things were underway. The flower delivery van was parked and workers hustled to get the delicate blooms out of the cold and inside. Adele parked and rushed over to assess their progress, and had a jolt of dismay when she realized the centerpieces for the reception weren't in the van. A quick phone call assured her they were coming in about an hour, in a separate van. Everything for the reception was being stored near the hall, so that the staff could do a quick turnaround with the room during the cocktail hour in a nearby lounge.

She stifled a sneeze and then reached into her bag for tissues. "Please, please kick in," she murmured, hoping the medicine she'd taken would help her symptoms and soon. She could be sick tomorrow. Not today. Twelve to fourteen hours was really all she needed.

Once the flowers were inside, she made a beeline for the spa to make sure everything was on schedule for the wedding party. That, at least, was going flawlessly. The bride and her bridesmaids were sitting in chairs, preferred drinks by their sides, having their hair straightened, curled, pinned…whatever their style required. The men, too, had appointments within the hour for hair trims and shaves. Everyone got to be a little pampered on the wedding day. The energy in the spa was warm and celebratory, and she smiled to herself as she left. The few hours leading up to the ceremony were some of the busiest, but also the most exciting.

Tomorrow would be time enough for a little self-pampering. She'd drink tea and stay beneath her very thick, very warm duvet for as long as she wanted. She always took the day after a wedding off as a treat to recoup from the long hours.

The centerpieces arrived and were properly stored. Adele lit the twinkle lights on the twelve trees. A small podium was installed for the justice of the peace, and the chairs were set up for the string quartet.

Her phone rang.

She hung up five minutes later, her heart

pounding. Four of tonight's servers had called in sick with the same flu. Four. With a guest list of two hundred and fifty, that made a huge difference. They were going to try calling in people who were off today, but with the virus going around, Adele wasn't hopeful. At least the photographer, Harper McBride, showed up early. Harper owned a studio in town and had quickly become Adele's go-to for weddings, as well as Adele's best friend.

Harper took one look at her and frowned, her blue eyes worried. "You're sick. You caught the plague."

Adele couldn't help but laugh, a welcome sensation that had been absent the last few days. "I did, yes," she admitted. "I was hoping it wasn't noticeable. I'm hopped up on daytime flu meds and a huge smoothie. Don't worry. I'll be fine."

"I know you too well. You look great, except the glassy look in your eyes. Well, darlin', the timing sucks." Harper lugged one of her bags into the room and hid it in a corner at the back, where she'd set up unobtrusively. "The place looks amazing, though. I think it's your best yet."

"Thanks." The praise went right to Adele's

heart. Harper had a brilliant eye and was also unfailingly honest. "Not too much white?"

Harper shook her head, which provoked one of her auburn curls to escape. "With that rich blue satin on the chairs and the silver accents? Not at all. It's gorgeous." She leaned a little closer. "I'm so glad you convinced her not to do the red."

Adele laughed. "Me too. Look, I know you have other stuff to do. I'll see you in here later, though?"

Harper nodded. "Yes, ma'am. I have the wedding-party photos to do, and all that 'day of' stuff. Do me a favor and go get yourself some hot tea. Mint or ginger or something."

That sounded delicious, so as Harper went on her way, Adele zipped to the coffee shop and put in her order. Just as she reentered the wedding hall, she noticed a delivery being unloaded that was all wrong.

She rushed forward, trying not to spill her tea and checking her phone for the time simultaneously. Instead she dropped her phone, held on to her tea and called out, "Stop!"

Everyone halted, but one delivery person got a strange look on her face. "Can I please put this down? They're heavy."

Of course they were. They were the ice

sculptures that weren't supposed to be delivered for another five hours.

"Why are you here now? The sculptures weren't supposed to be delivered until four o'clock." She bent and picked up her phone. The screen protector had cracked, but everything else looked okay. Thank goodness for small mercies.

"Our order said to leave at nine thirty. It's just over an hour's drive in our refrigerated truck." The apparent supervisor pulled out a folded paper and scanned it. "Look. Says here nine thirty."

Adele tucked the phone in her pocket and reached for the paper. It did say nine thirty, but she'd specifically asked for four o'clock, which meant a two thirty departure from the city. "We can't put them out now. They'll be melted before the ceremony! Even four was pushing it." The idea was for them to arrive at just the right time, so that they could be set up with the champagne within the reception configuration.

"I'm sorry, ma'am. But we've got another delivery today, and we can't take them all the way back to Calgary and drive back out again this afternoon."

She considered asking the kitchen staff if

there was storage space there. But these were three forty-pound blocks, shaped like snowflakes. Getting them from the kitchen to this room would be a challenge for the already understaffed crew.

Her phone rang.

They were still three staff members short for tonight's dinner service.

And she felt like crap—more so every minute.

Slow down and think, she reminded herself, trying to stem the feeling of panic crawling through her. She could handle this. It was her job. She handled anything that was thrown at her, right?

"Ms. Hawthorne?"

"Just a minute," she answered, trying to think.

Her phone rang again. When she hung up, she felt ready to cry.

Two members of the string quartet were down with the flu and so sick they were unable to play.

"Ms. Hawthorne," the delivery man said again. "What do we do with the sculptures?"

"I don't know!" she blurted out, and then let out a huge sigh. "I'm sorry. I suddenly have three crises and I need a moment."

She stood in the middle of the floor, wanting nothing more than to be back in bed. She was cold, she ached and she was simply *tired*.

Melting sculptures. Understaffed. *No music.* She knew bad luck came in threes, but she'd never had it happen at a wedding before.

"Is something wrong?"

She closed her eyes. Not Dan. This was the last thing she needed.

Take a breath. Smile.

She turned to face him and attempted the smile. "Oh, just some last-minute wrinkles I need to sort out."

He was frowning at her. "I get the impression it's more than a wrinkle."

"I can handle it."

"I know. So you've told me several times. But do you need help?" He stepped forward, his eyes earnest. "Sometimes handling it means delegating. But I'm sure you know that, too."

"The sculptures are hours early. They'll be melted before the reception even starts."

"A freezer in the kitchens?"

"I thought of that. But then we have to move them again…and we're down staff members. The flu."

"What about outside? On the balcony? It's

cold enough they'll stay frozen. We could ask if we can have a dolly and move them all back at once when they're needed."

"It might work. Let me make a call."

When she got approval to move the ice sculptures outside, Dan stepped in and helped load them onto the dolly, and then supervised delivering them to a corner of the balcony where they could come back and get them in the afternoon. Adele waited inside, where it was warm, but when he came back in, she ate a little humble pie. "Thank you, Dan. I was suddenly so overwhelmed. This is a great solution."

"About getting them back to the room and unloaded..."

"You'll have photos with the wedding party. Don't worry. I'll find someone. And if I have to, I'll get it myself. I can lift forty pounds."

He lifted an eyebrow. "Are you sure? You haven't started lifting weights, have you?"

She laughed in spite of herself and then covered her mouth. "No, though I do run quite often. Just not today. Today I'm in crisis-management mode."

"What else has gone wrong?"

"Besides not enough staff to serve tonight?

I've lost the string quartet. I don't know how I'm going to break that one to Holly. She's going to lose her mind."

"Probably." At her wide-mouthed expression, he shrugged. "It's her wedding day. I'm assuming she wants everything to be perfect."

"I don't know if I can get a substitute at this late hour. And I still have to find three more servers somewhere. I have an idea about that, but I have to clear it with the catering office first."

"Is there anything I can do to help? I'm off the hook until the before-wedding pictures at one."

Was he genuinely offering to help? It seemed he was. She gazed up at him, unsure of where she stood. "Last night we didn't exactly end things on friendly terms," she said.

"I shouldn't have said what I did at the end," he admitted, his gaze never leaving hers. "About the team player thing. It was a cheap shot. You're right. This is your job and you know what you're doing. I let personal resentment get in the way."

"I guess I'm glad that you're able to admit you resent me," she replied softly. "I prefer honesty over subtext. And I don't blame you,

Dan. I just…don't want to fight now. It was so long ago."

But was it, really? Clearly not if both of them were unsure of what to say or how they felt.

"The thing is, I want to keep on being angry. And I can't. I'm just…oh, hell. I don't know what I am. But I do know that my best friend is being married today and if his bride is unhappy, it's not going to be good for any of us." He smiled at her. "So, if there's anything I can do to help you out of your pickle, let me know. Hand me your phone."

She did, because she was too surprised to do anything else.

"There." He handed it back. "My number's in there. If you don't find a replacement for the quartet by noon, message me. I might have something up my sleeve."

"Thank you," she murmured, looking down at the phone and back up. "That's… kind of you."

He took a step back. "I might still be a bit angry with you, but it doesn't mean I want you to fail, Delly."

"No one calls me that."

"I can call you Adele if you want."

She swallowed against a lump in her throat. "It doesn't matter."

"If nothing goes wrong, I'll see you at the ceremony."

"Or before. I'll be taking the boutonnieres to Peter's suite before your photos. Those are the last flowers to arrive."

He gave her a mock salute and headed off down the hall, leaving her standing there, feeling unsure and off-balance. And only a little of that was because of her illness.

A brief discussion with the contract manager gave her the ability to bring in three additional servers, paid out of her own pocket. She called Emmeline and Jerry Richards, who owned a catering business she'd used often. They'd send three servers to the hotel by four o'clock so they could meet with the banquet staff ahead of time. Then she went to the bridal suite, where she faced a radiant and excited Holly.

"How is it? Is it all coming together?" Holly asked. "What do you think? The dress is still perfect, isn't it?" Harper was there, snapping pictures, and despite her growing fatigue, Adele went forward and adjusted the zipper and hook at the back of the dress.

"It's lovely. And it is all coming together, with one hitch."

Holly's face fell. "Oh, no. Is it bad?"

"It's nothing I can't handle, but it's big enough you need to be aware. Your string quartet has backed out. Half of them are down with the flu." And apparently not as amenable to working while sick as she was.

"But...that's all the music!" Her voice raised with panic. "That's what I'm supposed to walk up the aisle to!"

"I know," Adele said, feeling a little panic herself but keeping calm for the sake of the bride's sanity. "I've got calls in to a few replacement ensembles that I've worked with before. I'm hopeful, because January isn't a busy wedding month. We might be lucky."

"And if we're not?"

Adele reached out and took her hand. "I have never let a bride down yet, and you won't be the first."

"Okay." Holly let out a breath. "I'm going to trust you with this, Adele. Please, please make it work."

"Everything else is ready, and your flowers should be on their way up in the next thirty minutes. The weather is perfect, too, so don't fret." She sent a reassuring smile. "I've pulled off miracles before."

She left the suite and rested against the wall

after the door was shut. Keeping a bright face had been a big chore. She needed to take another dose of pills soon; the fever and chills were worsening, and her whole body ached.

Her phone dinged with a text message—the quartet she'd used before was already booked for this evening. That only left one option. If they weren't available...

She grabbed a bottle of water, but then stopped and got a bowl of soup to get her through the day. The warm broth helped her throat, which was feeling a bit raw, and revived her a bit. Until she got the final refusal. They were two and a half hours from wedding time and had no music. Holly was not the sort of bride who would want a recording played for her walk down the aisle, either.

Desperate times called for desperate measures. She tapped in a text message to Dan, asking for his help. By the time she'd finished her soup, he'd messaged back, saying that a pianist and flautist would be there and set up by two thirty, and if guests could wait until after that to be seated, it would allow them a few minutes to warm up.

She hadn't wanted to rely on him, but he had come through anyway. Just like he always had when they'd been together.

Her heart ached a bit thinking about it. If she'd told Dan she'd been diagnosed with cancer, he would have stood beside her. If she'd told him it had spread to her uterus and she had to have a hysterectomy, he would have held her hand and insisted it would be all right.

And then she would have had to face him every day, feeling responsible for denying him the joy of his own children. Wondering if he would grow to resent her as his siblings had children and they remained childless. If he'd regret staying with her all that time, and if he'd eventually stop loving her.

The way her dad had stopped loving her mom.

Dan was still a good man. And he had come through today, helping her out of a jam. But nothing had really changed.

Nothing at all.

CHAPTER FOUR

DAN HAD GLIMPSED Adele briefly when she'd dropped off the boutonnieres to Pete's suite, but she'd slipped in and out again so quickly, he hadn't had time to speak to her. Her cheeks had looked flushed, though, and her eyes strangely bright. He supposed it might be because everything was coming down to the wire.

As he and the groom and other groomsmen stepped out of the elevator, the muted sound of piano and flute touched his ears. He let out a sigh of relief. A Calgary colleague had a daughter studying music and it had only taken one phone call and the promise of a generous last-minute fee to arrange something. They were almost to the doors of the hall when Adele came around the corner, her phone in hand.

"Whoa," he said, reaching out and grabbing her arms to avoid a collision.

She looked up, dazed. "Oh, gosh, sorry!" Her cheeks flushed a deep pink. "I didn't even see you…all." She looked around at the rest of the men. "But this is perfect timing. You all know what to do, yes? And we're just about ready to open the doors and begin seating the guests."

"Pete and I will hang back and go in with the JP," Dan said, letting go of her arms.

"Yes, that's perfect." She smiled a little. "Everything is finally coming together. The last few minutes can get a little manic, though the idea is to appear as if everything is tranquil and calm."

The groomsmen headed for the main doors, and Pete saw someone he knew and sidestepped to say hello.

Dan looked down at her and frowned a little. Her eyes were brighter than normal, and not in a good way. He lifted his hand and touched her forehead. "Oh, my. You're sick, aren't you?"

She swatted his hand away. "Don't say a word. I'm doing okay. It's just a touch of… something."

"The timing is horrible."

"Don't I know it." Her face softened, though, when she looked up at him. "Dan, thank you for the assist earlier. The soloist is just perfect. How did you know who to call?"

He was more pleased than he should have been at her gratitude, and it didn't settle well. "The guy who moved to Calgary to set up the satellite office, his daughter studies music. I gave him a call, she was available and brought an accompanist, and there you go."

She smiled at him, a genuine smile. Maybe she was delirious. "You make it sound like no big thing, but it totally saved my butt today. And I'm not in the habit of it needing saving."

"I'm coming to realize that. Anyway, I'm glad I could help." He had to stop looking into her eyes. It made him forget how much he resented her for walking away. "Pete's a good friend, and Holly's a sweet person. They deserve their fairy-tale day."

And he would not be bitter about it. Just because he'd been prepared to propose after graduation...it hardly mattered now. Clearly it wasn't meant to be.

Her phone vibrated. "Call?" he asked.

She shook her head. "Alarm. It's time to get you with Ms. Fraser, and time for me to head upstairs for the bride and bridesmaids."

She turned to leave but he put a hand on her

arm. "Are you really okay? Considering people are dropping like flies with this bug..."

She looked at his fingers for a moment, and then looked up into his face. For a fleeting moment, something passed between them. Not regret, not awkwardness. If he didn't know better, he'd swear it was longing. But that didn't make any sense. *She'd* left *him*. And never looked back.

"I've been drinking lots of tea. It helps."

"Okay," he responded. There was nothing — to be done, anyway. The wedding would go on and she was stubborn enough to power through. He'd learned last night not to bother insisting on anything. Adele was far more stubborn than he remembered.

The next time he saw her, she was standing by the door of the hall, cradling an actual mug instead of a paper cup. He moved into position at the front, standing next to Pete, while the ushers took their places to his left. She took a sip and then put the mug down on a small table at the back, rolled her shoulders and gave the flautist a nod.

When the opening bars of Gounod's *Ave Maria* sounded, she slipped out the door.

Then the doors opened—both sides—and the first bridesmaid entered, her hair perfect, smile wide, her navy dress rippling along the carpet runner. Then the next bridesmaid and the maid of honor, all carrying identical bouquets of mostly white blooms with silvery accents. Looking around at the twinkly trees, flowers, chairs and other preparations, Dan started to understand exactly how much planning went into a wedding day, and how Adele had taken Holly's vision of her magical day and made it a reality. A new respect for her blossomed. She was good at this. Really good.

The music changed, shifting to Pachelbel's *Canon*, and Holly stepped inside the doors.

A collective gasp went up from the guests, and one glance at Pete told Dan his best friend was a goner. Pete's hands were folded in front of him, but Dan saw the fingers clench and release several times as Holly started her walk up the aisle. And when Pete's eyes misted over, Dan reached inside his pocket and took out a pristine white handkerchief. When he handed it over, an emotional laugh fluttered across the room, making the vibe suddenly very warm and personal.

He looked to the back of the room and saw Adele standing there, a satisfied smile on her face.

He gave her a brief nod before turning back to the ceremony.

And yet, as the people he cared about said their *I dos*, as he handed over the wedding band and signed the register, he couldn't stop a hole from opening in his chest. This should have been them. It *would* have been them, if it had been his choice. And maybe it was better this way. Maybe she'd known something he didn't, and they wouldn't have lasted. Not getting married had to be better than going through with it and divorcing later.

But for the first time in several years, he came face-to-face with the fact that he'd never gotten over her. And now he wasn't sure if he ever would.

Relief was the only emotion Adele felt right now.

She had twenty-five whole minutes during the ceremony to sit down at the back of the room, out of sight, and sip her tea, which was miraculously still hot. One of the waitresses for the cocktail hour had noticed her sniffling and had brought her a fresh cup, a very thoughtful gesture and one of the reasons Adele loved having events at the Fiori

Cascade. Luca, Mariella and their team did a fabulous job.

But once she got through her mental checklist for the ceremony, making sure nothing needed the smallest tweak, she found her mind wandering to Dan.

His help and concern today had been utterly unexpected, but he had backed off instead of pressing the issue like he had last night. Of course, he'd made it plain he was doing it for Pete, and not for her. Still, he didn't have to. And then that moment when he'd put his hand on her arm…there'd been something. Something that was impossible to ignore, even though she knew she should.

But again…she'd never stopped caring about him. So maybe she should stop thinking and just give herself a break. It was natural for feelings to crop up, wasn't it?

Dan handed the ring over to Ms. Fraser and then stood back, clasping his hands loosely in front of him. He was still so handsome, too. And when he'd grabbed her arms this afternoon, stopping her from colliding with everyone, he'd smelled the same as she remembered.

I've got to be delirious, she thought to herself. She was spending far too much time thinking about the best man when she should be thinking about the next steps the moment the ceremony ended.

But sitting down had been a bad idea. Now she felt as if a fifty-pound weight was tied to her feet, and she didn't want to get up. Exhaustion started to creep up on her, and she knew that was a bad thing. A few more hours were all she needed. Once dinner was served, once the cake was cut and the first dances over with, everything else would just play out. The guests would enjoy the open bar and the music, the happy couple would retreat to the honeymoon suite, and that was that.

A few hours. She could make it.

But first, she had to stand up.

She got to her feet and made a point of draining the mug of honey lemon tea. The flautist was playing something simple now as the bride, groom and witnesses signed the register. It would only be a few more minutes and they would walk out of the hall as Mr. and Mrs., and Adele would zip up to the lounge to ensure the cocktail hour was ready to go.

That she was feeling weaker by the moment didn't help matters. At all.

But she persevered, mentally pushing

through by reminding herself she could sleep all day tomorrow if she wanted to. She dashed to the lounge to ensure the champagne was chilled and the bartender ready, as well as the waitstaff who would circulate with hot and cold hors d'oeuvres. She slipped out of sight as all two hundred and fifty guests made their way past the wedding party. Immediate family would stay behind for pictures.

Once the hall was clear, Adele and the Cascade staff leaped into action. The whole room was reconfigured, adding tables and moving the chairs around them, and then topping the tables with navy and white linens. Adele blew her nose and then reached in her bag for hand sanitizer before helping place the centerpieces on each table. Place settings were added. A tech crew came in and adjusted the microphones and added a podium for the emcee and speeches. The potted trees were moved for a more precise placement and the showstopper, the champagne table, was wheeled in and prepared.

Which meant that it was time to bring in the sculptures.

Adele checked her watch. It was ten minutes to five—perfect. The doors would open to the reception at five thirty, giving the ice an hour more time than initially planned. The man with the dolly seemed to have disappeared and the setup staff were clearing away the unnecessary items, so she retrieved the dolly herself and pulled it to the glass doors leading to the patio. Three sculptures. She could handle that. Better to get started now than waste time searching for someone to help. Forty pounds was nothing…or at least, normally nothing. Today she thought it might as well be a hundred, but she'd manage. So far, so good.

The air was frigid, and bit through her cashmere sweater as if it was nothing. It didn't help that she hadn't grabbed gloves. Her shoes squeaked as she walked across the stone, little bits of snow stuck in the mortar. Three sculptures. It wouldn't take long and she'd be back inside, toasty and warm again.

The first icy square was manageable, but just. She grunted as she lifted it onto the dolly, and when it was secured, she stood, stretched her back and caught her breath. Her heart pounded unusually fast, disproportionate to the exertion it would normally take to heft that much weight. A shiver ran through her and she shuddered, feeling the sudden urge to cry. Why did she have to be sick, today of all days?

She was just reaching for the second block when a pair of hands appeared beside her. She looked up to see Dan, his breath frosty in the air, coming to assist. She shouldn't let him, but the help was so welcome that she took a step back. "What are you doing out here?"

"Photos on the patio. Right now it's just Pete and Holly, and I saw you come out." He lifted the sculpture as if it weighed nothing and placed it on the dolly. "Are you crazy? You're sick and you don't even have a jacket on."

"I know," she admitted. "I'm in get-it-done mode, but it's freezing." She reached for the last sculpture, determined to show him she was fine. But she lifted, stood and everything went woozy.

"I got it." He took the weight from her hands. "I'm guessing you don't want to drop one of these."

"They're not big, but they sure do cost a lot," she admitted. "Thank you again, Dan. You keep running to my rescue. Normally that'd make me mad, but today I'm just grateful."

He put his hand on the handle of the dolly and started pulling it toward the doors. "You're really sick, huh?"

She nodded. "I feel worse now than I did this morning. But we're nearly there." She tried a laugh as she opened the door for him. "I can manage."

They got inside and he unloaded the ice blocks to their spot on the table. She knew she shouldn't read too much into his actions today, but he really had gone above and beyond.

"Dan, I mean it. Thank you. I know we… That is, it's…"

"We don't need to talk about it," he said, his voice sharper than before. "It's over and done with."

The teamwork vibe of only moments before was obliterated with his terse reply.

"Look, I've got to get back out there. You've got this. I'll see you later."

He spun on his heel and disappeared back out onto the cold patio, leaving frost in his wake.

CHAPTER FIVE

SHE WAS EVERYWHERE.

Dan had hoped that Adele would disappear once the reception started, but he saw her here and there, flitting about, adjusting the microphone for the emcee, switching place cards at the last minute, supervising servers.

He sat at the head table with the other members of the wedding party. The mood was celebratory and he did his best to join in and not bring it down, but it was hard with reminders of Adele all around him.

He picked at the watercress and arugula salad, barely tasted the soup. When his main came, a delicious-smelling plate of stuffed chicken and asparagus risotto, he made more of an effort. He looked over at Holly, whose face was alight with happiness. Pete leaned over and kissed the crest of her cheek. Dan reached for his glass of wine and took a sip, and then wished for something stronger.

He'd stepped in to help Adele several times, and he kept asking himself why. She certainly didn't need rescuing, and he didn't owe her anything. He might pass it off as simple good manners, but he knew that would be a lie. He refused to label it further, but it annoyed him just the same.

He'd nearly finished his chicken when Adele came forward and knelt between Pete and Holly's chairs.

"Sorry to bother you," she said softly, "but I was wondering if you'd like something else to drink, Holly? I noticed you haven't touched your champagne. Is it okay?"

"Oh." Holly was turned slightly toward Dan's side of the table and he could see her face. Her cheeks colored and she looked to Pete, who grinned.

"I might as well tell you," she answered quietly. Dan could barely hear her. "We were waiting until after the wedding to say anything, but since you noticed I'm not drinking… We're expecting."

Adele's face paled and her knuckles whitened around the rungs of Pete's chair. But she recovered quickly and smiled brightly. "Oh, that's lovely news! Mum's the word, I promise." She laughed a little, but Dan had known her long enough to know it wasn't quite her genuine, heartfelt laugh. "Mum's the word. Get it?"

Awkward. That was the only way to describe the moment. He didn't know what to do, either. He'd never noticed Holly abstaining during their other meals together, but it was easy enough to assume a mixed drink contained alcohol.

Pregnant.

Adele pushed herself to standing again and smiled. "In that case, I'll just make sure your water is topped up, unless you'd like something else."

"I'm fine, really." Holly couldn't contain her smile. "And thank you, Adele. You were right. Today has been perfect."

"I'm glad. I'd better disappear into the woodwork again. Just shout if you need anything."

She disappeared out a side door, but not before he saw her pale face or the shadows beneath her eyes. He wasn't sure if she'd taken more meds, but she was clearly feeling worse by the minute.

But it wasn't his problem. Not in the least.

CHAPTER SIX

ADELE WASN'T SURE she could stay on her feet much longer.

The meds were no longer working. After persevering through the day and fighting valiantly, she was quickly starting to lose the battle. What she needed was to go to bed, to curl up in her cozy blankets and attempt to sleep this off. She prayed the virus didn't last long. She had a Valentine's Day wedding coming up, plus she hated being sick. Even a simple cold or flu made her uneasy, as if her body were somehow betraying her. It had been this way ever since her diagnosis and treatment. Being sick made her feel weak… and out of control.

She watched as Holly and Pete had their first dance, and tried to keep some emotional distance. An hour and a half ago they'd been clients. Lovely clients, certainly, but she hadn't felt quite like this. The news that Holly was pregnant had somehow flipped a switch inside her. And it wasn't as if she'd never had pregnant brides before, though not often.

She rather suspected it was because Dan had been right there, looking at her. That he'd been in her little sphere of existence for the last two and a half days, bringing up all sorts of memories and feelings.

Happy-ever-after. That wasn't what she promised, but she did ensure that couples got off to a great start. She bit down on her lip as Holly and Pete rested their foreheads together, their feet slowly shuffling to the sweet song. They were clearly in love, had a gorgeous home outside Calgary with a view of the mountains, and a baby on the way. A perfect little life.

Dan stood on the edge of the dance floor, watching them, too. For a moment, his gaze flitted to her, and then away again. He hadn't said a word to her since she'd stopped at the head table. The day was nearly over, and she didn't need his help anymore. It was crystal clear that his assistance earlier hadn't been from any lingering...affection, perhaps? Nostalgia? He seemed to be doing a much better job of keeping his emotional distance than she was. It was getting harder and harder to ignore the ache in her heart each time she saw him or heard his voice. That laughing timbre had once been just for her. The way he rubbed a finger over his eyebrow when he was deep in thought hadn't changed. All the little things that had been out of sight, out of mind, were suddenly right before her eyes.

One of the staff members came by and offered her a piece of wedding cake. The smell of it turned her stomach; she hadn't eaten since earlier in the afternoon and the medication, plus copious cups of tea, had her tummy not quite settled. Her head pounded and the loud music wasn't helping. At this rate, she was just going to leave her car here tonight and get a cab home. Getting behind a wheel simply wasn't a good idea, nor did she want to expend the energy required to focus on the road.

She sneezed into her sleeve, and then reached into her pocket for a tissue. Again.

The first dance ended, and she persevered through the next few numbers, where the wedding party and family joined the couple. As soon as the obligatory pairings were over, she made her way over to Pete and Holly. She made sure she didn't get too close; the last thing Holly or Pete needed was to get sick on their honeymoon.

"Everything's well in hand. Congratulations, you two. I'm going to be heading out now."

"You're not staying until the end?" Holly's face fell, and Adele's heart warmed.

"You don't need me now. The bar's open and running smoothly, the hotel staff has everything under control and the DJ is here until midnight." She paused and then decided to be honest. "Truthfully, I've come down with the same bug that created some of our staffing issues today. I've been popping cold-and-flu pills since this morning, but I'm really starting to feel awful. Plus, I don't want to give it to anyone, including you two."

"Oh, Adele! You should have said something earlier!" Holly sounded genuinely distressed.

"It's fine. I promised you a day of your dreams, and I hope you had it."

"We did," Pete said. "Everything was beautiful. Not quite as beautiful as Holly, but amazing."

She smiled, though her head was pounding in time with the upbeat song blaring through the speakers. A shiver racked her body. "I'm sorry. I'd love to stay. I just…"

She weaved for a moment, light-headed, and reached out for a chair to steady herself.

"Adele," Pete said, his voice deep with caution. "You *do* need to go. Thank you for everything, but please, go look after yourself."

She nodded, but then Dan's voice came from behind her. "Is everything okay?"

Adele turned to say yes, but Pete interrupted first. "Adele is horribly sick. You can't drive," he said to Adele, and then looked at Dan again. "Could you see she gets into a cab, Dan?"

"Of course."

Dan took her elbow and she followed him meekly, too sick to put up any sort of a fight. The momentum of the day had kept her pushing through, but now that it was over, it seemed she'd lost all her fight. They stopped to get her coat and bag, which she was certain he carried out of politeness. They were outside the ballroom, where it was cooler, when she tugged on his arm.

"Wait." She couldn't keep up with him. Plus, the cooler air felt so good on her face, even though her body was cold. Her heart was racing, too. "I feel weird, Dan. I need a minute."

"Take the time you need. I'll let them know we need a cab."

"I need a cab," she corrected him, but he was already gone.

Even the thought of dragging herself to bed seemed a monumental task. She sat on a nearby chair, but when Dan approached, rubbing his hands together, she stood. Too quickly. Everything around her blurred and swam.

"Adele!" She heard him call out, but it sounded as if his voice wasn't connected to his body. Instead her knees wobbled and she started a slow slide...

When she came to, they were in the elevator and she was cradled in Dan's arms. "What happened? Where are we going?"

"You fainted, and we're going upstairs. I'm not letting you go home like this."

She struggled against his arms, but they tightened around her. "I can't stay here. Put me in a ca—ha-*hachoo*!" She sniffed.

"Stop fighting. You're in no shape to go home. I don't know how you made it through your day. You're burning up."

The elevator dinged and she wondered how

strong he had to be to hold her in his arms for so long.

"I can walk."

But he ignored her as he stepped out into the corridor of the quiet floor and started down the hall.

"Dan…" She tried to twist a little. "I don't want to give this to you."

"I've had my flu shot."

"That doesn't mean you can't get sick. What if it's a different strain?"

"Well, you were probably contagious yesterday, so it's too late anyway. It's going around. You're probably not the first person I've been exposed to." He frowned down at her. "I take it you didn't have your shot."

She shook her head. "I kept meaning to…" It was stupid, really. Someone like her, who hated being sick, should have been first in line for this year's vaccine.

He did put her down when they got to his door. He reached into his tux pocket for his key card and swiped it. "Come in."

She stepped into his hotel room. She'd been in the rooms here before, several times, and they never failed to impress. Dan's room was done in cream and gold, with a window overlooking the valley and mountains beyond. He went to the window and pulled the drapes, and then to his dresser, where he took out a pair of boxers and a T-shirt.

"Here. Can you manage to change without fainting again?"

It was said with concern, not venom, and his eyes were clearly worried. She touched her cheek; it flamed beneath her fingers. "I think so."

"Don't lock the door. You scared me when you fainted."

The fact that she even had the power to frighten him made her insides twist with unease. She shouldn't be here. Not in his hotel room. She sniffled again, so without answering, she went into the bathroom, blew her nose, and slowly changed out of her sweater and trousers and into the boxers and oversize tee.

They smelled like him. Worse, his scent was just the same as it had been eight years ago. A woman didn't forget, and Dan's unique scent was intrinsically tied to her memories.

When she came back out, he'd opened a bottle of water and put some in a glass for her. "Do you have any medicine left?"

She nodded. "In my bag. But they're not helping."

"The acetaminophen might at least help with the fever and aches."

God, yes. The aches.

He retrieved her bag, and she got out the bottle of pills and then dutifully drank all the water as she took two. She couldn't stop shivering now, particularly since the T-shirt and boxers were not exactly warm.

"Here. Get into bed." He turned down the covers and she slid inside, sighing as he covered her with the soft sheet and duvet.

"Oh, God," she said, closing her eyes. "It feels so good to be off my feet. This bed is… Oh, it's bliss." She burrowed deeper into the covers, the mattress so comfortable, she wondered if she would ever want to get up.

"You should have gone home hours ago," Dan said quietly, sitting on the edge of the bed. Her eyes were closed, and she sighed when his fingers grazed some hair off her face and tucked it behind her ear. The simple touch was incredibly soothing.

"Are you going back to the dance?" she asked, her breath deepening. "You're the best man. You should go back."

"Sure," he replied, but his voice sounded far away. "You just get some rest."

Her breathing started to deepen… The bed

was just so comfortable, and even though she was still shivering, she was far cozier. "You're the last person who should be looking after me," she murmured.

"I know."

His voice was soft. Not quite accepting. Resigned? Her heart ached at the thought. Regret seeped through her, knowing she hadn't been fair to him all those years ago. She'd hurt him, deeply. For good reasons, but it didn't erase the result.

"About when I left, Dan…"

"Not now. Get some sleep. You need it."

She felt the bed lighten as he got up, heard a door open and then close again. Then she heard nothing at all as she fell into sleep.

Dan wiped a hand over his face and watched Adele shift beneath the covers, still sleeping.

He'd spent the night on the cramped little sofa in the sitting area of his room, with a spare blanket from the closet. He hadn't really minded; despite his conflicting feelings for Adele, she was definitely sick and had fought to hang on throughout the day, like a complete professional.

Seeing her start to collapse in the lobby had sent his heart to his throat. He'd just caught her before she crumpled to the floor, and then lifted her into his arms. It had been a bittersweet sensation, holding her close like that. It brought back memories, good ones. When they were younger and silly and so full of each other. She hadn't really changed, either. She fit in his embrace just as easily as she had all those years ago.

He hadn't gone back to the reception. He'd been genuinely worried about her fever. She'd been burning up, and weak enough that she'd fainted. Leaving her alone had seemed cold and unfeeling, so instead he'd gone into the bathroom, taken a long, hot shower, pulled on a pair of sweats and tried to get some sleep. Her sneezing woke him a few times in the night, as well as some random mumblings he couldn't make out. The talking in her sleep was a new development, and he'd fought to understand the garbled words. He'd come up blank, though. She'd been pretty incoherent.

He still wasn't sure what meeting up with her again was supposed to mean. Closure? Maybe. He certainly hadn't been able to make a relationship stick since she'd left. Wouldn't it be something to be able to get some answers to his questions and finally leave her behind him?

She mumbled in her sleep again and his brow furrowed. This didn't feel like closure. *It felt messy.*

He ordered up some breakfast and dressed in jeans and a sweater. Today was a wedding party "tea" off-site, very casual, and a way to wind down the celebration before Pete and Holly left for their holiday in Jamaica. By then, he'd probably have Adele back home and he could say goodbye.

The thought left him feeling oddly bereft.

A knock at the door announced room service, and once the cart was delivered and he'd tipped the server, Adele began to stir. She'd been asleep for nearly twelve hours.

"Dan?" Her voice was raspy. She pushed her hair out of her face and sat up a bit. "Was that the door?"

"I ordered some breakfast."

"What time is it?"

"Half-past ten."

She still held the covers close. "I slept all the way through."

"You did." He poured her some orange juice, took it to her and then sat on the bed. "Here. Drink this." As she sipped from the glass, he touched her forehead. Still hot, though perhaps not quite as hot as last night. The sleep had done her good.

"That's so good," she said, finishing the glass of juice. She shivered. "I don't know why I'm still so cold."

"Because you're not well yet. You're just… better." She didn't look better, though. Her eye makeup from yesterday was smudged, and her hair was puffed up on one side. But the glassy look was gone from her eyes, at least.

"I should get going…"

She went to pull back the covers, but he was sitting on them. "There's no need to rush. I ordered you some tea and toast. Scrambled eggs, too, if you want some."

She laughed, and then started to cough a little. "You and your eggs."

He shrugged. Friday, when she'd remembered how much he liked eggs in the morning, he'd been taken aback. Not just that she remembered, but that she'd actually mentioned it. Her eyes had lit up with that little bit of mischief he remembered. They'd been together for three years. A lot of memories had been made—ones he couldn't erase no matter how much he tried.

"We can eat and then I can take you home, if you like."

Her face changed, the easy expression replaced by awkward tension. He hadn't meant it to sound like he was trying to get rid of her, but he could tell that was how she'd taken it.

"I'm okay to drive today. I still feel like I was hit by a bus, but it's better than last night."

"Whatever you want, Adele." He softened his voice, trying to keep the tense energy in the room from escalating. "But eat something first." He poured her tea. "And have some tea."

She accepted the cup and thanked him. "I swear, I've had more tea in the last few days than I've had in a month."

"It's good for you. That and chicken soup."

"That's an old wives' tale."

"Not true. There's actual science behind it." He came back to the bed, took her mug, set it on the nightstand and then put a plate in her hands.

"Raspberry jam. My favorite."

It seemed she wasn't the only one with a good memory. He'd remembered she preferred raspberry to strawberry, and grape jelly ahead of both.

She started to eat, and their conversation ceased. Dan started to feel more and more awkward. Last night she'd been so ill and tired, he'd merely tucked her into bed. Today he didn't know what to say or do. She would be walking out of his life again in probably an hour or so. They'd say goodbye and that would be it. She'd go on with her life; he'd go on with his. And this weekend would become one of those "remember that time you ran into your ex at our wedding?" memories he'd share with his friends.

So why did it feel so…wrong? Like there was something left he was meant to do?

He went to the dresser and got the remote for the TV. An old *Friends* rerun was on, and he flipped through a few channels until he got to some type of home improvement show on the Home and Garden Television network.

"Dan?"

He turned around and she was standing there, dressed in his boxers and T-shirt. His mouth went dry. Despite the smeared mascara and wild hair, Adele was still a beautiful woman. Her curves were hidden beneath his clothes, but he knew they were there, and even though she wasn't a tall woman, her legs seemed to go on forever.

She put the plate on the cart. "Thank you," she said quietly. "For looking after me last night. I was in no shape to drive. You could have put me in a cab and you didn't."

"You'd fainted. I didn't want you to be alone."

"That was big of you. Considering...well, considering how much you must resent me."

He did. And yet he didn't. It was easier to hate someone when they weren't standing in front of you. Easier to reduce them to a two-dimensional "character" in your life than a flesh-and-blood, flawed but sweet woman.

"I don't resent you," he said, knowing it was only a half-truth. "It's just awkward because we have history."

Awkward. Another massive understatement. Truthfully, spending time with Adele yesterday had reminded him of some of the things he'd really liked about her. She was smart, efficient, capable, funny, compassionate. Her one flaw was not wanting to be his wife.

Maybe he needed to finally get over that.

CHAPTER SEVEN

ADELE KNEW SHE should change out of Dan's clothes and go home. It was the sensible thing to do. And yet…she couldn't. Not yet. Because this would really be the end, wouldn't it? Walking away hadn't been easy then and it wasn't now, either. Because this time she was sure he wouldn't be back. The moment she went through his hotel room door, that was it.

"What is it?" he asked, coming to stand in front of her. She'd been quiet for so long that concern wrinkled his brow. "What's the matter?"

She met his gaze. "The whole 'we have history' part. This whole weekend has been strange and it's like we've danced around the whole topic of our past. It feels…unfinished."

The worry cleared, but she noticed the barriers he'd erected to keep her out were still in place. His gaze was distant, impersonal.

"There's not much to tell. You didn't feel the same as I did, and you left."

The words were a knife to her heart. "Yes, I suppose that's how it looked. How it...must have felt."

Cold eyes locked with hers. "How it felt? How about it felt like you'd ripped out my heart and stomped on it, then handed it back to me and told me to have a nice life? Some of those dents don't pop back out, you know. They're permanent."

"I'm sorry, Dan. I wasn't good at breaking up with you." She bit down on her lip. Loving him had been the easy part. Leaving had been horrible.

"Then why did you?" He backed away, reached down and fiddled with a fork that was on the room-service cart. "I've gone over and over it in my mind, Adele. It never felt right, that your feelings just up and changed like that. Not that I'm perfect, but..." He put down the fork and sighed. "It was so out of character for you. It made me wonder if everything that was 'us' was really a lie. If it had ever been real, or if I'd just wanted it to be."

She walked over to the window and looked outside, her chest aching at his last words.

She'd loved him, all right. More than she'd thought possible. Which was why she'd wanted to spare him the pain that would follow.

When they'd been together, she'd lived in an apartment close to campus, with a view of downtown Toronto. The view that greeted her this morning was that of snow-covered mountains, blue sky and evergreens so dark, they were nearly black. Worlds apart. Maybe she should just tell him the truth and get it over with. Maybe he would understand.

Maybe she finally would, too. Because what had seemed like an obvious choice eight years ago suddenly seemed less sound.

"It wasn't a lie," she said quietly, resting her hand on the window frame. "None of it was a lie, Dan."

"Then it just doesn't make sense. And it makes me angry all over again." His voice came closer, and she knew he was standing behind her. Chills shivered up her spine and along the back of her neck that had nothing to do with her illness.

A lump lodged in her throat in response to the rawness of his voice. "Maybe I should just go."

He sighed. "It might be easier. Best. Something."

She escaped to the bathroom and hurriedly changed out of his clothes and back into yesterday's trousers and sweater, already missing the spicy man-smell. A glance in the mirror had her reaching for a cloth to wipe the smeared eye makeup off her face, and she scraped her hair back with her fingers, wishing for a hair elastic to tame the wild strands. She smoothed it as best she could, but the lump in her throat wouldn't shift.

Guilt. That was what she felt. Guilt at lying and guilt at leaving. And she wasn't sure if telling him the truth would make him feel better or worse.

When she left the bathroom, he was standing by the window, in the exact spot she'd vacated. He looked lonely and unapproachable. Had she done that to him? She'd considered her actions a kindness and had told herself that repeatedly over the years when thinking of him. But now she was wondering if it had been a convenient way to avoid accepting the hurt she'd caused.

"You hated me, didn't you? And you still do."

He shrugged, but didn't turn around. "I wanted to, and that's enough."

But he hadn't. And oh, that hurt, too. But what could she say? That she was wrong? That she'd made a horrible mistake? It had been the right thing, breaking it off. Nothing had changed, had it? Except he still didn't have that big family he wanted, despite her setting him free.

Why?

"Thank you for looking after me last night," she said softly. "It was more than I deserved."

He spun around. "You keep saying things like that, and I don't understand. It's like you're telling me one thing and meaning another. Just like the day you walked out. Cut the subtext already and just say what you mean."

"I... I can't." No one here knew about the cancer or the hysterectomy. Not even Harper, who'd become her best friend.

Dan's lips were a thin, angry line. "Then maybe you should go. We always had honesty between us, Delly. Right up until that last month. I knew something was wrong, but you wouldn't tell me. I thought maybe it was that we were graduating and you were unsure of the future." He laughed, a bitter, sharp sound. "I thought if I proposed it would be okay. But instead you dropped me like a hot potato. That's when I figured you'd met someone else. I can understand you not wanting to admit it back then, but for God's sake, you could at least have the guts to be honest now."

His words bit into her like a bird's beak pecking relentlessly against her skin. She wasn't one for crying, but tears pricked at the corners of her eyes and the lump in her throat tightened to the point of pain.

He had been going to propose.

She didn't reply. Instead she stumbled toward the bed, grabbed her coat and handbag from the floor, and then headed for the door.

"Delly...wait."

The plea in his voice sent the tears spilling over her lashes.

She kept going.

Adele slept for two hours that afternoon, and then went back to bed again at eight and slept through until Monday morning. When she woke and rubbed her eyes, she realized it was still dark out and checked her phone on the nightstand. Barely seven. She coughed, a dry-sounding hack that hurt her chest, but the worst of the congestion was gone.

Her cat, Mr. Num-Nums, was curled up by her feet, his black tail wrapped around his fluffy black-and-white body. As she moved, he lifted his head and blinked slowly, and then with a little chirpy meow, he hopped up, made his way up the bed to her belly, put his paws just above her belly button and started to knead.

She laughed. "Good morning, bubby," she crooned, and reached down to rub his ears. "You kept my feet warm all night, didn't you?" He'd been very vocal when she'd returned home yesterday morning, demanding to know where she'd been all night. She'd had just enough energy to refill his food and water before heading for the sofa and a blanket.

He gave up kneading and perched on her belly, rolled his head a few times, and then flopped down. His antics never ceased to make her laugh, and the warmth of his body had kept her from feeling lonely many nights.

She was probably a crazy cat lady, but she didn't care. Mr. Num-Nums was her fave.

He started to purr and she put her head back down on the pillow. Today she had to ignore the fact that Dan was still in town, and instead had to get back to work. The Valentine's Day ceremony at Lake Louise was in just over three weeks; details were starting to come together and needed her attention. While winter wasn't her busiest season, she had two weddings coming up that were destination weddings and required a different sort of attention. And then when April hit, her busiest season would kick off from then until October, really.

There were things she needed to do now, including putting things together for her accountant for tax season.

But for right now, her bed and cat were warm and comfy, and she was going to enjoy a few more minutes.

Shortly after eight she dragged herself out of bed, hopped into a hot shower, and dressed in soft, comfy leggings and a cozy sweater. She'd bought hand-knit wool socks at a market in the fall, and she pulled them on to her feet before heading to the kitchen to brew coffee—not tea.

In moments the coffee was dripping into her mug, and she popped two slices of bread into her toaster. Daylight started filtering through the windows, and she pulled open the blinds before feeding the cat.

Then she set up her laptop at the kitchen table, close to the coffee maker and the heating vent, and started answering the emails she'd ignored for the past forty-eight hours.

It was all very normal, except she couldn't get the sound of Dan's voice out of her head. Or the strange feeling in her stomach that was at once excited and nervous and also heavy with regret and dread. He made her feel so many things.

But he was going back to Toronto in a few days. Back to his life. And she'd continue on with hers. If she was left feeling as if things were unfinished—well, that was her own fault. As her mom used to say, *If you burn your ass, you have to sit on the blisters*. She'd made her choice, and now she had to live with the fallout. Again.

She made another cup of coffee, and then a knock came at the door at precisely noon. Her heart hammered as she wondered if it was Dan. But a quick peek through the little window showed Harper's face amid a cloud of her breath. Adele opened the door and stood aside. "Hey. I didn't expect to see you today."

"I gave you time to sleep. And thought you

could use this." She held up a bag from their favorite lunch spot. "Chicken soup."

"That sounds awesome. Come on in."

Harper used her toes to push off her boots and left them on the front mat. Stocking-footed, they headed back to the kitchen. "Well, I wanted to be nosy, too. Last I saw of you was when the best man was walking you toward the door. He's kind of hunkalicious, don't you think?"

She must have winced because Harper's eyebrows went up. "What? Is he a jerk? What happened?"

"You'd better sit down. Want a coffee? I'll get a spoon for the soup. Have you eaten? Is there some for you, too?"

"That's a lot of questions," Harper replied, pulling out a chair. "Yes, I'll have a coffee. And yes, I ate and the soup is just for you. Now. Spill."

Adele popped another coffee pod into the machine and hit the button. "Well, I didn't have time to tell you this on Saturday, but… the best man's name is Daniel Brimicombe and he and I were in a relationship a long time ago."

"Shut up. Really?"

Harper had swiveled in her chair so that she

could face Adele. The look of surprise was priceless. Adele put milk in the coffee and brought it and a spoon to the table. "Really. In university. We broke up just before graduation."

"But why? Like I said, hunkalicious." She wiggled her eyebrows.

Adele laughed a little, despite the little knot of pain that centered in her solar plexus. "I know. I couldn't believe it when I saw him at the hotel. What are the chances? Anyway, our relationship didn't end well, so the weekend was pretty awkward."

Understatement of the year.

"It didn't look awkward when he was helping you to the door."

Adele wasn't sure how to respond. She reached into the paper bag and took out the carton of soup, avoiding Harper's penetrating gaze.

"Adele?" She said her name slowly, and Adele sighed as she took the lid off the soup and dipped her spoon into it.

"Actually, he didn't take me to the door." She put a spoonful of broth in her mouth and affected what she hoped was a casual air.

"Oh, sister." Harper leaned back in her

chair. "There's a story here. You might as well let me have it."

Adele sighed and met Harper's gaze. "You're right. And I probably should talk about it rather than overthink everything."

Harper leaned forward. "Did he kiss you?"

"With the virus I had going on? Are you nuts?" Adele laughed. "I'm sure my fever and sneezing were really attractive. No, I fainted, actually. Dan took me up to his room and tucked me into bed with some medication. Then he went back to the dance."

Harper took a drink of her coffee, but one eyebrow was quirked in a sassy arch. "Nope. He never came back. Why else do you think I'm here? I saw him take you out and then didn't see either of you for the rest of the night, and I stayed until nearly midnight." She sent Adele a knowing look. "I didn't pop by yesterday in case he was…you know, here."

Adele frowned and spooned up some soup to cover her conflicted feelings. He'd stayed with her? The thought that he'd watched over her sent a warmth flooding through her body. It also made her uncomfortable, considering the conversation they'd had the morning after.

Yet despite his feelings, he'd stayed. Made sure she was all right. It was a reminder that he was a good guy, deep down. Even when he was mad.

"I didn't realize," she said finally. "I fell asleep right away and slept through until the morning." She swallowed against a lump in her throat. "He slept on the couch."

"Not exactly the actions of someone who hates you, Adele."

"It's complicated."

Harper finally laughed. "It always is. You wanna talk about it?"

And get into the nitty-gritty details? Not really. She was still feeling quite raw from it all. "Thanks, but it's all in the past, you know? And he's only here for a few days. I won't even see him again."

She'd no sooner got the words out of her mouth than there was another knock at her door.

A delivery man stood on the step and held a fruit basket in his hands. "Are you Adele Hawthorne?"

"I am."

"This is for you. Have a good day."

"I don't need to sign?"

"Nope."

He was gone in a flash and she carried the basket inside and to the table.

"Oooh. Fruit." Harper sat back and watched as Adele reached for the envelope with a small card inside.

Adele,
Thought you could use the vitamin C. I'm sorry about how we left things. If you're feeling better, maybe we can meet for lunch this week?
Dan

Adele wasn't sure what to think. It was an olive branch, she supposed. And she probably shouldn't read much into it. After all, it was bananas and grapes and not a bouquet of flowers or chocolates, the typical romantic go-to.

"Well? Is it from him?"

She nodded. "Actually, yes."

Harper sat back with a satisfied smile. "See?"

Adele undid the cellophane and took out a fragrant clementine. She started to peel it and forced a shrug. "It's fruit, Harper. Not exactly romantic."

"Right. It's subtle. Slipping in under your radar."

She couldn't help it; she laughed. "He's not an under-the-radar guy. Or subtle, really. He's more tell it like it is." She didn't mention anything about the lunch request. It had been nice talking to Harper, but the details were still a sore spot that she didn't care to share. *I don't have a uterus* wasn't really something you popped into a conversation.

Harper drank her coffee for a minute and Adele ate some sections of clementine, the fruit juicy and fresh.

"Did you really love him?" Harper asked, and Adele nearly choked.

She coughed for a minute and then took a breath. "Sorry. I guess I'm not quite over my bug yet."

"Well, did you? Was this a big deal?"

She could lie, but what was the point? "It was," she admitted. "Throughout most of university. We were together three years."

"That's a long time."

"He was going to propose." The words slipped out before she could stop them. Harper's eyes widened, and Adele bit down on her lip. "I didn't know that until yesterday. But I... Our lives were going in different directions. I knew letting go was for the best."

"And you broke his heart."

And my own, she thought, but kept the words inside.

"Regrets?" Harper asked, reaching into the basket for a handful of plump green grapes.

Did she have regrets? A week ago she'd have said none. But now, after having seen him, after being face-to-face and remembering everything, she wasn't so sure. "I don't know. It's been hard seeing him. I thought leaving him was the right thing to do, but it still hurts."

"And now he's back here."

Adele nodded. "Just for this week. I'll be fine. I have work and the cat and it's all good."

Harper took the grape stems and her cup to the sink. "Well, I need to get back and finish touching up the photos from the wedding. But you call me if you need anything, okay? I mean it. We can do girls' night in or go out or just…whatever."

"Thanks, honey. And for the soup, too. I appreciate it."

"I know. Otherwise I wouldn't do it." Harper chuckled and gave Adele a hug. "Take a nap. You still don't look a hundred percent."

"Yes, Mom," she replied.

Harper was gone in a whirlwind, the way

she seemed to do everything. But once the door shut and all was quiet again, the smile slipped off Adele's face.

What did a fruit basket mean, exactly? And how was she going to answer his invitation?

CHAPTER EIGHT

HE WAITED FOR her in the bakery/café, wondering if they'd still be able to get one of the small tables by the time she arrived. They could always go somewhere else, but he was nervous.

He shouldn't be. It was Delly, after all. He knew her better than he'd ever known anyone, really. Well, he knew the person she'd been back in Toronto. The new Delly looked the same but acted differently. She was more efficient, more…subdued. Serious. Maybe they'd simply grown up.

He checked his watch again and sighed. Yes, he was early. But that didn't make the waiting go any easier.

He saw her through the window before she came through the door and his heart gave a solid thump in response. It had been like that each time he'd seen her over the past several days—that traitorous, initial reaction that said he'd never gotten all the way over her. Then his brain would catch up and remind him that she'd broken his heart. But that first glimpse...it reminded him of when it had been the two of them against the world, making plans and laughing in the dark.

She came through the door, cheeks rosy from the cold, her eyes brighter and more alive since the last time he saw her. The flu seemed to have run its course. She smiled at him, her eyes made bluer by the pale blue of her thick scarf. Lord, she was pretty.

"Hi," he said, smiling back. "Thanks for meeting me."

"No problem," she answered, unwinding the scarf from around her neck. "It's a great choice for lunch."

A table opened up and they snagged it before anyone else had a chance. "Busy," he observed.

"It's a tourist town, and this is ski season. You get a blend of locals and visitors in here. Tourists for lunch, locals for the baked goods. I'll be leaving with a loaf of sourdough."

They ordered sandwiches and drinks and he looked at her again. How could she be so relaxed when he was in knots? "You look recovered," he said.

"I slept most of Sunday and into Monday. Thank you for the fruit basket, by the way. And my friend Harper—the photographer from the wedding—brought me soup. I took it easy and ate well and now I just have a lingering cough. Nothing serious. It was short but nasty."

"You scared me to death when you fainted." Watching her eyes roll and her knees buckle had made his heart miss a beat. It had only taken a second to lunge forward and catch her. Wise or not, there was no way he wanted her to go home alone when she was clearly so ill.

Their drinks came and he lifted his cup. She did the same, took her first sip, and then put it down and met his gaze evenly. "So, why did you ask me here, Dan?"

He swallowed the hot liquid and regretted it, as it burned its way down his throat. He coughed and reached for his napkin, and then his water glass. When he looked up again, her eyes were twinkling at him. She'd enjoyed his discomfort and he couldn't really say he blamed her. He'd kind of put her on the spot with the invitation.

"I wanted to apologize. Things got heated Sunday morning and I didn't like how we left things." He paused, turning his coffee cup around in a circle on the table. Then he looked up again and admitted what had been on his mind for the last two days. "When we broke up, it was very...acrimonious. I didn't want to do that this time. If we're going to say goodbye, I would like it to be on friendly terms."

At her confused look, he amended, "I mean, *when* we say goodbye, of course."

"Of course. Because you're only here until..."

"Sunday night. Then a stop at the Calgary offices for a few days and back to Toronto."

Five more days. He had plans for some skiing and hiking, plus a soak in the hot springs. It had sounded relaxing and somewhat idyllic just a week ago, in the few days before the wedding. Now it was colored with facing Delly again and the tug-of-war of wanting to know the truth and knowing it would probably be better to stay away.

She sipped at her water instead of reaching for her coffee. "So, you asked me here to... what? Apologize? Extend an olive branch?"

"I lashed out on Sunday morning, and it

was unfair. Particularly since you were feeling so rotten."

Their sandwiches came and they halted their conversation as the waitress put the plates down on the table and asked if they needed anything else. When she was gone again, Dan tried once more. "I blamed you back then for ruining my life. Of course you didn't," he hurried to assure her, and he meant it. He had a good life. A great career. Nothing was ruined, but rather just tarnished. "I have a good life. I'm happy."

"So you've said," she replied, her face unreadable.

"And I started blaming you again when I saw you last week in the lobby of the Cascade. The truth is, you left and you must have had a good reason, and me lashing out is just a case of...pride."

Well, that and a wounded heart, but he wasn't going to bring that up again.

"I see," she said, this time reaching for her coffee. She lifted the cup and he frowned a little. Was she hiding behind it? The foam at the top jiggled a little, as if her hand was shaking. Was it? Was she more discomposed than she let on?

"You did have a good reason, right?" he

asked, toying with a pickle slice on the side of his plate.

She put down her cup. "I did, Dan. I promise I did. And I know I hurt you, but truly it was to save you more pain down the road."

Quiet surrounded them again. When it was clear she wasn't going to elaborate, he defiantly picked up his sandwich and took a bite.

He assumed it was delicious, but the flavor was a bit lost on him now that things had turned awkward. He'd give anything for things to be, well, easier between them again. It would probably never happen, so he finished half his meal before looking up at her again.

Tears shimmered in her eyes as she bit into her sandwich, chewed and swallowed so thickly it looked painful.

His heart seemed to plummet right to his stomach. Crying? Delly? She rarely cried. Never really had. He'd only seen her cry twice before. Once when they broke up, and once at Christmas, when her mom had been going to drive down to Toronto from Sudbury and hadn't made it because of weather. She'd grown up the very independent child of a very independent single mother and wasn't

prone to tears. That she was so close now un-
manned him.

"Delly," he said gently, ignoring his "pride"
and reaching across the table. He circled her
wrist with his fingers and she put the sandwich back on the plate. "What is it? I didn't
mean to upset you."

She shook her head, and two small tears
were shaken loose from her lower lids. They
dropped down her cheeks, and she gave a
small sniff and then cleared her throat. With
her free hand, she reached for her napkin and
dabbed her cheeks.

"Does this have to do with the reason you
left?" he asked, hesitation making his throat
tight.

"I can't talk about it. Not here." Her voice
was a strident whisper, pleading with him to
change the subject. But he couldn't, not yet.
He had to know one thing first. Something
that had weighed on his mind ever since that
awful spring day.

"Was there someone else, Delly? Did
you fall out of love with me and in love
with someone else? I've wondered all these
years—"

But his words were cut off by Adele rising abruptly, grabbing her jacket off the back

of the chair and rushing outside, leaving her lunch half eaten.

He sat for a moment, unsure of what to do. Go after her? Maybe, but was her exit a tacit admission? What if she had regrets? What then? And he couldn't just run out without paying the bill. He didn't have cash on him, so he got up from the table and approached the counter, suddenly weary. He'd wanted to apologize. To leave things less acrimonious than they'd been. Instead he'd upset her and made things worse than ever.

It seemed to take forever for the woman behind the counter to ring through his debit card. He pocketed the receipt and headed out the door, not hopeful he'd see Adele. She was probably long gone by now. He pulled his phone from his pocket, considered sending her a text, but then put it back. Usually he was decisive, making important decisions and following through without second-guessing. But with Delly, it had never been easy. *Why was that?* he wondered.

Hands in his pockets, he walked down the street toward the small parking lot at the edge of the park. He was nearly to the museum when he saw the flash of her scarf, a bright bit of blue in the white-and-gray day. She was walking, but her arms were wrapped around her middle, as if protecting herself from the cold...or something else. He'd upset her again. And he was beginning to understand that the only way to break the pattern was to hash out the truth once and for all.

Throat tight and heart pounding, he set off to catch up to her.

Adele huddled into herself as she made her way over the snow to...somewhere. A bench, the gazebo, maybe. The air was cold and not many people were wandering the park today, all either in the shops or on the ski hills. She just needed to keep walking. To let the bite of the winter air jolt her out of the idea that Dan thought she might have cheated on him. And yet, what was he supposed to think, when she'd never explained? She couldn't blame him, but it still hurt.

The gazebo was empty; the day was too cold for many people to be sitting outside. But not her. She'd welcome the frigid temperatures. Maybe punishing herself would somehow make her feel better.

"Adele."

Her body tensed as Dan's voice echoed

behind her. She should have known he'd come after her. There was simply no escaping him this week. The pit in her stomach grew heavier. She was going to have to tell him. It was the only way he'd give her some peace. And the only way she'd have peace, too. Years of avoiding it had allowed her to push the memories to the back of her mind. Almost as if it had never happened. Looking forward, rather than back.

There was no avoiding it now. Denial was a fickle witch.

His boots sounded on the gazebo steps and he made his way to the bench, sitting heavily beside her.

And said nothing. Just sat there, his elbows on his knees, probably with thoughts racing through his head, as they were in hers. Wondering what was the right thing to say.

She looked out over the Bow River and sighed. "There was no one else, Dan. I promise. I didn't love anyone..." Her voice caught a little. "I didn't love anyone but you."

His breath came out in a whoosh. "Is it wrong that I've wondered all this time?"

She shook her head, still not looking at him. "No, of course not. In the absence of information, we create our own. Or at least our own doubts." Her heart sank. "I'm starting to wonder if I did the right thing after all."

She could feel his gaze on her profile. "You mean breaking up?" he asked, and she wondered if he sounded a little breathless or if that was all in her head.

"No," she admitted. "But not telling you why. The real reason why."

She looked over her shoulder. The park was still mostly empty, save a few tourists around the perimeter. She and Dan were blocked by the wind inside the gazebo. She laughed a little, a bitter sound that bit into the frosty air. "Do you know I've planned weddings that took place right here in this gazebo? It seems so strange right now."

Dan just waited, silent. Words collected in her throat in a jumbled-up mess of justifications and excuses, but she couldn't make herself say them.

Finally, she let out a breath and chanced a look at Dan. His jaw was set and he looked so…unhappy. Not angry, not sad. Just unhappy, and the time had come to be honest.

"Dan, there's a lot I need to explain. If you can just wait for me to finish, instead of interrupting me, it would help. I think I need to get this all out in one go so you understand."

He met her gaze. "Still setting conditions," he said quietly. "But all right. If you couldn't be honest then, and it upsets you so much now, I guess it must be a big deal."

She nodded. Clutched her fingers together inside her mittens in her pockets. "Okay…"

A quick swallow, an inhale and she finally said the words she'd kept from him for so long.

"In March of our last year of university, I had a checkup at the doctor's because I'd been having weird period symptoms. I'd never had a pap test before. We'd been together since first year, no other partners. I was young. But it came back abnormal, so I went for a biopsy, and it came back positive for cervical cancer."

She heard his sharp intake of breath but plowed on, determined. "Finals were coming up. We were graduating. But I was so distracted. Meanwhile your family was planning grad events and talking about the prospect of new babies in the family and I… I just saw you in the middle of all that and got so scared."

He looked up at her and opened his mouth, but she held up a hand. "Not yet," she cautioned. "Let me finish. I had scans. Visits to the oncologist, and a treatment plan. Surgery…

scheduled for May, after grad. They were hopeful they could just do a simple procedure. But then a scan showed more tissue involvement, and I was scheduled for a hysterectomy."

"A hysterectomy?" Dan did speak up then, his voice breathless with shock. "My God, Delly. You kept this all to yourself?"

"Wait," she pleaded, not wanting to get to this part of the conversation yet. She had to get through the medical stuff first. "I knew what the surgery meant. No children for me. Not ever. I asked if there was a way around it, but no. Hysterectomy was the only way. The follow up treatment—radiation—would possibly harm my ovaries, so it was suggested that I harvest some of my eggs and freeze them. I didn't. I was twenty-one. What was I going to do with frozen eggs? I wouldn't have a uterus to carry a baby, anyway."

She looked over at him, trying to ignore the stricken look on his face. "Your family is so big and happy. Your parents couldn't wait for grandkids. Your sisters were already talking about starting families. For God's sake, your mom had blankets crocheted for future grandchildren. I already felt intimidated when we were with them, coming from the background I did. I didn't have siblings or a big happy family…and I saw your face every time your cousins came over with their little ones. Having a family was so important to you. And it was something I could never, ever give you."

She hesitated. It was out. Nearly all of it. Her stomach was a mess of nerves, tangled and painful. Saying the words out loud transported her back to those days, sitting alone in the doctor's office, her stomach already feeling empty and…barren, even before the surgery.

"Did you think I'd leave you?" The edge in his voice was sharp. "Is that how little you thought of me? That after three years, I wouldn't stand by you? Did you even know me at all?"

He jumped up from the bench and paced to the railing. A pointed curse left his lips and he hung his head. "You lied, Delly. You stood in front of me and told me you didn't feel the same as you used to. That we were better off apart." He swore again and ran his hand through his hair. "I can't even… My God."

"I didn't lie," she said quietly, her fingers clenched so tightly now, they hurt. "I meant every word I said. I didn't feel the same because *I* wasn't the same. I wasn't in charge of my own damned body, don't you see? Bits and pieces of me were going to be cut away. Everything changed in those moments! Everything! And while the prognosis was good, in every cancer patient's mind there comes a moment when they wonder if this is it. Or if a recurrence will hit them from nowhere. Learning I would never have children was devastating enough. But I faced my mortality, Dan. When I was barely more than a kid."

"You didn't have to do it alone!"

Her breath hitched. "I know. I knew you would stand by me. You would have gone to every appointment and been there when I woke up from surgery. And I knew that every time I'd look in your eyes, it would be with the knowledge that I could never give you the family you wanted. And that one day you would resent me for it. Hate me, maybe. I couldn't stand that. You...you needed to be with someone who could give you all the things I couldn't, so I set you free."

"Free? You think I've been free?"

The anguish in his words tore through her gut. "Haven't you been? You've dated. You've been free to marry someone, have children... Don't you still have those options?" Frustration bubbled up and then out of her mouth.

"At least you still have those options, Daniel! I don't. I never will."

Silence fell in the little gazebo. A couple who was walking along the river path had stopped and looked up when they heard her raised voice, and now resumed their stroll.

"I'm sorry," she apologized. "I didn't mean to shout. It's just… I left because I thought doing so was the kindest thing I could do for you. Just because I couldn't have a family didn't have to mean that you couldn't."

"You might have told me why."

Oh, the bitterness. It sliced into her like she always knew it would, but perhaps this was like lancing an old wound. At some point, you had to let the crappy stuff out so it could heal properly. It was an ugly, messy business.

So she inhaled, exhaled slowly, got up and walked to where he stood. She put her hand on his arm. "I thought about it. And I knew you'd try to change my mind. Insist it was no big deal and we could deal with it together. And I'll confess, you probably would have been able to convince me. It was so painful, leaving you. The only thing that kept me going was knowing that I was giving you a…a gift. The chance to have the kind of life we never could together."

"You don't see me having that life now, do you?" he asked, the bitterness still ringing in his voice. "Do you want to know why? Because I don't trust anyone. I get just so close and then I break it off before they can leave me. That's what you did to me, Adele. Some gift."

He made a scoffing sound and turned away. She bit down on her lip and fought back against the tears that threatened. "That wasn't my intention," she murmured, her breath forming a tiny cloud in front of her face. "I was twenty-one, Dan. We were so young. I'd never had to navigate a relationship like ours before. And cancer changed everything. It seemed like a lot to ask of a guy who was just getting his undergrad."

"So you made the choice for me. Nice."

"Can you please try to understand my feelings on this?"

His gaze snapped to hers. "I can't understand anything right now. I'm still trying to make sense of it in my head." He started to back away. "I need to go. I'm going back to the hotel. I need to think. I'm sorry, Adele."

Back to Adele—not Delly. He was upset. Angry, certainly. And probably confused. She'd had years to think about this, and he'd just had it all dumped in his lap.

"Of course. I understand."

Two words. Two words she'd wanted him
to utter, but knew now he never would. He'd
never understand why she'd made the choices
she had. And he probably wouldn't forgive
her, either. But now it was all out in the open.

He spun on a heel, jogged down the few
steps of the gazebo and took off across the
white expanse of the park, his steps quick
and purposeful.

Adele stood there for a while, watching
him go. Eight and a half years ago, he'd had
to watch her walk away. And now it was her
turn.

CHAPTER NINE

THE HOT SHOWER did nothing to wash away the mess of emotions roiling through his head and stomach.

Delly couldn't have children.

She'd lied about why she was leaving him.

God, she'd gone through that all alone.

She'd taken the choice away from him when he hadn't even realized there was a choice to be made.

The last two were the ones that hurt him the most. That she'd unilaterally made a decision that would affect both their lives without even considering he should have a say in it hit him square in the gut. A part of him had wanted to ask, "Who do you think you are?" but he'd held it inside, the words jumbled together like a mouth full of marbles.

And then there was the fact that she'd had cancer and had been all alone through surgery, recovery, radiation...had she had chemo, too? He didn't know. Through the fear and uncertainty and days that she must have felt so ill. He couldn't get the images out of his head—her on an operating table, hooked up to an IV for chemo. Her hair...had it fallen out?

And he'd been off with his friends and family, angry as a mad hornet, nursing his emotional wounds.

If only she'd told him. Trusted him.

He toweled off and pulled on a pair of jeans and a sweatshirt. What was he going to do now? Sit in his hotel room for hours, doing nothing? Why had he thought a week alone was a good idea? The idea of spending the rest of the week here by himself was no longer alluring. It was just...lonely.

What he should do is pack his stuff and head to Calgary, spend a few extra days in the office and then go back to Toronto. Leave all this behind him.

He pulled out his suitcase, put it on the bed and then went to the drawers of the dresser and started taking items out. He'd finished with the dresser and had moved on to the closet when a knock came at his door.

He paused, his hands holding a sweater

about eight inches from the case. Holly and Pete were off on their honeymoon. Unless it was staff, there was really no one except...

Adele. She knew which room was his. She'd slept here, for God's sake.

He put the sweater on the bed and moved to the door. He looked through the peephole, and sure enough, there she was, her face red and her lips a little puffy, as if she'd been crying. He closed his eyes for a moment and considered not opening the door. He could pretend he wasn't here. Avoid having another disastrous conversation.

There was a raspy sound by his feet, and he looked down to see a slip of paper slide under his door. It was face-up, and simply had the words "I'm sorry" written on it.

What a mess. What a horrible, horrible mess.

He opened the door.

She'd turned to walk away, but swiveled back at the sound of the door opening. He stood there, meeting her eyes, and wondered how a love that had once been so simple and straightforward was now so complicated and painful.

Cancer, he realized. If it hadn't been for the cancer, he would have put a ring on her finger.

He held out the paper. "I know you're sorry."

She came back, her steps cautious and her red-rimmed eyes wary. "I didn't want to leave things like we did this afternoon." She took the paper from his fingers. "And we've said that to each other more than once this week. Do you think we could...?" She halted, her lower lip wobbling a bit. "Do you suppose we could get it right this time and go our separate ways without one of us getting super angry?"

He stepped back and opened the door wider, a silent invitation for her to enter.

She stepped inside, but halted by the door and looked at her feet. "Should I take off my boots? I don't want to track snow and dirt onto your carpet."

"Sure," he answered. What else was he going to say? Even now, as she bent over to unfasten her boots, he kept picturing her in a hospital bed. He hadn't been there. And he hadn't because she'd shut him out. That hurt him more than anything.

She stood straight again and spied the case on the bed. "You're packing." Her lips turned down in a frown.

"I was, yes," he agreed, going back to the bed. He tossed in the sweater, closed the lid and placed the case on the suitcase rack near the closet. "Banff is suddenly feeling very small. I thought I'd spend a few extra days in Calgary. Check out the new offices. See how things are going there."

"I see."

His gaze met hers. Lord, she looked so sad. A part of him wanted to reach out, fold her into his arms and tell her it was okay. The other part wanted to shout at her for not giving him a chance to be the man she'd needed.

"Dan, I…" She hesitated for a moment, but then seemed to find her words. "I'm just so sorry. About all of it."

"We were young. And you were in a highly stressful situation."

She nodded, looking relieved. "I was. Looking back, I can see how maybe I shouldn't have made such big decisions in that state of mind. I just knew how much you wanted kids. How big your whole family is on it, and I pictured us as the one couple without any. It seemed so unfair to you."

He nodded, trying to stay calm. "I should have been in on that decision, though. You understand that, don't you?"

"I… I was afraid I'd give in, you see," she said quietly. "That you'd convince me it didn't matter. You'd say all the right things and I'd love you even more, but then…you'd start to resent me. It would kill our relationship. And that would have killed me, you know? To have more of you. To believe in…forever. I couldn't. I was just…afraid."

She took a step forward. "I was afraid of everything. And so I isolated myself." Her lips dropped open. "I never realized that before. I cut myself off from everyone. Not just you. Everybody."

He understood what she was saying, even if he didn't agree with it. And he wasn't a heartless jerk; he could see she had anguished over it. However angry he was—and had been—he knew this was not something she'd done without thought or feeling. "We would have supported you. Been there for you."

She nodded. Her lip trembled.

"Aw, hell," he murmured, and did what he'd promised himself he wouldn't. He pulled her into his embrace and held on tightly.

Adele let out the breath she'd been holding at the feel of his arms around her. This was wrong, so wrong. It would just add to the confusion. But since he'd shown up here last Thursday, nothing had been straightforward. She'd been fighting the memories of the past—not just of their relationship and breakup but those horrible, horrible days before and after, when she'd faced the grim reality of illness, recovery and loss.

And she'd turtled. Withdrawn into herself. At the time, she'd thought she was reserving her strength. Focusing. But that wasn't it. She had been fighting but she'd also been running away.

Now she wondered if she'd ever actually stopped running, or just set up her life so that there was nothing to run *from*. Simple. No attachments other than Mr. Num-Nums.

"I'm sorry, Dan. I'm so sorry."

"What for?" he asked gently. "It's not like you asked to get sick. Or wanted this to happen."

"For hurting you. For maybe making the wrong choices, even if they were for the right reasons." Her voice was muffled against his shoulder. "For not being strong enough."

He put his hands on her upper arms and pushed her away a little, then bent his knees so they were eye to eye. "Don't say that again. You're one of the strongest people I know. Misguided, maybe," he added, a small smile, curving his lips. "But never weak."

"Oh, I'm weak," she said, swallowing hard. "I ran away." And weak because she was loving the feel of his fingers on her arms just now. Had loved being in his arms just moments ago. It was a sensation both exciting and familiar. How many times had he held her when things had gotten tough? When she'd feared she'd bombed a midterm or paper? When she'd caught a horrible cold just before Christmas finals? Or even just simple things, like spilling a cup of coffee or stepping in a puddle, soaking her foot? His arms had always been there.

And she'd thrown that away out of fear. Telling herself it was best for him, but really afraid that she would never be enough to make him happy.

He took her hand and led her to the little sofa. "Come and sit down. I think we've finished yelling at each other. Do you want some tea? Some food? You hardly touched your lunch."

She shook her head. "Though if you want to make coffee in your little machine, that would be fine."

"Sounds good."

He readied the water and coffee pod and she took the few moments to steady herself.

When he came back over with a cup fixed the way she liked, she smiled up at him. "Thank you. For hearing me out. For not hating me."

He turned away to make his own coffee, but his voice reached her just fine. "I haven't walked in your shoes, Delly. I'll admit I was angry. Am still a little angry, to be honest, but that's because I was…am…shocked. I'm trying to put myself in your shoes. What would I do if I got a devastating diagnosis? And the truth is, I just don't know. So I'm trying to wrap my head around it and not judge."

He came back to the sofa with his coffee and sat beside her. "All I can say," he continued, "is that the thought of you being so sick and alone hurts me, right in here." He made a fist and placed it just below his breastbone. "And I'm so sorry that you can't have children. I know you wanted them."

The want wasn't exactly in past tense; Adele still got twinges of pain and sadness whenever someone she knew announced a pregnancy or had a new baby. She'd got better, though, at accepting her reality. There was no sense wishing things were different, because they would never be different.

"Thank you," she said quietly. She wanted to reach for his hand but didn't; there was making peace and then there was…being too intimate. Instead she cradled her cup and inhaled the rich-scented steam. "But there's still time for you. I know you want children. Your face, when you told me about your nieces and nephews…you lit up. There must be a special woman back in Toronto."

He turned his head and his gaze caught hers. "No," he admitted, "there's not. I mean, I've dated, but it's never been serious. Not like…that," he finished.

But she wondered if he'd been going to say "us."

The room was quiet, too quiet after his statement, and the silence filled with something new, or perhaps something old that was renewed. She found herself staring into his eyes, her lungs cramping as she struggled to breathe. Attraction. Now that the anger and fear were gone, there was room for old feelings to be resurrected. And that scared her horribly.

She turned away and took a sip of her coffee, while Dan cleared his throat, pushing the moment away.

She stayed for an hour, answering his questions about her illness. All the things she should have told him years ago and hadn't.

It was difficult, but when it was over, she felt better, stronger. Holding it in, never telling anyone…it hadn't been good for her, she realized. In a way, she'd been living her life holding her breath. Working at a job she loved but always with this *thing* hanging over her.

And yet, in another way, it brought the truth right to the surface again, and it hurt.

The afternoon was waning, and the sun had long since disappeared behind the mountains. She brushed her hands down her jeans and stood up, letting out a big breath. "I really should go. I meant to work this afternoon, and I didn't. I can catch up on some things tonight. Besides, you probably have plans." She looked over at him as he stood, too. "Are you still going to leave and go back to Calgary?"

He shrugged. "I don't know. It was a knee-jerk reaction because I was frustrated. I don't feel the need to blast off like I did earlier." He smiled a little, and it sent a little beam of light into her heart. He always did have a great smile.

"It's a nice city."

"It is, but I'd still be there alone. I guess there are some people in the office, but…"

"But this was supposed to be a vacation."

"Yeah."

She moved to the door, grabbing her coat off a chair as she went. "I don't remember when I last took a vacation. Any time it's high travel or tourist season, it's also high wedding season."

"Understandable." He picked up a glove that had dropped from her coat pocket onto the floor and handed it to her. "But how about playing hooky? Do you ever do that?"

She laughed. "Not really. It's not my style. I just tend to take Sundays off."

"After the wedding, time to recoup?"

She nodded, shoving her arms into the sleeves of her coat.

He stepped closer. "Play hooky with me to-morrow. I know it sounds crazy," he added. She'd snapped her head up in the middle of zipping the zipper, surprised at his offer. "I want to go skiing and I don't want to spend the whole day alone. You do ski, don't you?"

She did, and hadn't gone more than once all season. But a day with Dan? She laughed. "What, today's emotional roller coaster hasn't been enough for you?"

He smiled again. "I know. It's weird. But it might be nice to spend some time together without either being angry or apologizing for something. No strings, Delly. Nothing heavy.

Just a day on the slopes. The weather's supposed to be good and it's midweek. Shouldn't be too crowded. At least I'd have someone to talk to on the lifts."

It was tempting. Very tempting. She'd made it out once in December and that was it, which was a travesty considering the world-class hills all around her. And he was right. It wasn't like they'd actually talk much, except on the lifts back to the top.

"Where are you going?"

"I don't know. Either Sunshine or Lake Louise."

Her two favorite hills.

But this was Dan. The man she'd once considered to be The One. The man whose presence had tortured her for nearly a week now.

But also an old friend. And they'd used to enjoy the outdoors together.

"Okay. One day of skiing, only because I haven't been out all month. But that's all the time I can afford to take off. And only because it's sad to think of you doing that all alone."

His smile widened.

"I knew you'd take pity on me. Do you want to take the shuttle bus? I know it leaves from the lobby entrance in the morning."

She shook her head. "No, let's take my car. I've got a rack on the top. I can pick you up around nine if you want."

"Sounds perfect."

He held open the door for her and she stepped into the hallway. "I'm glad we talked, Dan. It feels so much better."

"Me too. It was hard. Hard for you and hard to hear. But I'm starting to understand. I'll see you in the morning."

She walked down the hall, a sense of unease following her. Maybe he was starting to understand, but she wasn't sure she was. Because this afternoon seemed to change a lot of things, and she didn't quite know how to feel about it.

Adele arrived at the hotel a few minutes before nine, her skis strapped to the top of the car and her poles and boots in the back. She waited out front, wondering if she should text Dan that she'd arrived when he strode out the door, looking like an ad for winter sportswear. Her pants and jacket were good quality, but Dan's were top of the line. He held a cardboard tray with drinks in his hand, a small paper bag nestled between them. A pair of goggles rested on the top of his hat and a string bag was slung over his shoulder. When he saw her car, a smile brightened his lips.

Her heart thumped in response. Not in a million years had she thought she'd be spending a day on the slopes with her ex. It just went to show that life was unpredictable.

He opened the car door and slid inside. "Perfect timing. I saw you pull up just as I was getting coffee." He handed her the tray to hold while he fastened his seat belt. "Thought we could use it for the road. Where are we going?"

"I thought Lake Louise. I went to Sunshine last month. It's not a long drive."

"I haven't been there since I was a kid, and it was summer."

"I can take you to the Chateau after if you like, if you want to see the glacier and the lake."

"Maybe. We'll see how the day goes. I haven't been skiing for a while." He put the cups in the cup holders, and then tapped his legs. "These might give out before the end of the day."

She doubted it. Even though he had ski pants on, she knew the thighs beneath were strong. Like the rest of him. She'd gotten a good look the morning after she'd stayed in his hotel room.

She sipped on her coffee as they reached the highway and headed west. The drive really wasn't very long, and it was beautiful. He broke off pieces of walnut muffin and handed them to her, and they talked about skiing and other noncontroversial subjects until they reached their destination.

Parking was close to the lodges at the bottom, and Dan hit the pro shop to rent his equipment, while Adele took her skis off the roof rack and slid into her ski boots. They met out front of the main lodge. Dan's cheeks were rosy from the brisk air, but it was a beautiful day for rushing down the slopes, just a few degrees Celsius below freezing and the barest of breezes.

"You ready?" she asked, flopping her skis down on the snow and then stepping her feet into them with quick snaps.

"I am. I'll let you pick the run since this is my first time."

She considered for a moment. There were days that she was brave enough to tackle some black diamonds, but Dan only skied occasionally and she wasn't sure of his level. "Let's go up the express and warm up with a green run. Then we'll see, okay?" One thing she particularly liked about this hill was the abundance of long, leisurely runs. There were lots of beginner and intermediate trails that ran from top to bottom.

They got on the lift and then off again at the top, taking a moment to enjoy the view. "God, it's gorgeous up here," he said, letting out a big breath. "Like you're on top of the world."

She laughed. "There's a lift that goes up higher, actually. And another on the back bowl. There's a green run to go down the back side, but black diamond on this face." She wiggled her eyebrows. "Not sure I want to tackle that today. Anyway, let's go down this one." She pointed to the green sign. "I have to find my legs before I get too crazy."

He laughed, put down his goggles and away they went.

She'd needed this badly, she realized, as she made graceful turns down the groomed trail. There was something about the rush of speed—not too much—that was exhilarating, and the fresh air that made her feel free and strong. Dan was just ahead of her, his form only slightly shaky with his knees a bit wide but firmly planted over his skis. He moved with confidence, and she was glad. A day of blue and green runs would be fun. Maybe an expert level thrown in before the end of the day, before their legs got too tired. Her cough had dwindled to the occasional scratch, and her energy was back. She attributed her recovery to sleep and power smoothies.

They reached the bottom with a final swish and a laugh. "Oh, that was really nice," she said, putting up her goggles. "A few centimeters of new snow last night made the trail just right."

"You're not a powder girl?"

She shook her head. "I always find it too unpredictable. I get a bit of a rhythm going, then hit a puff of powder and the change in speed throws me off. I don't enjoy it as much."

They took the lift up again, and took another trail down. Then a different lift and some other trails, until Adele wondered what time it was. She hadn't brought her phone with her on the hill because she didn't want to fall and chance breaking it. Dan had left his in the car for the same reason, so on their next trip to the bottom, they took a break at the lodge and went inside to check.

It was twelve thirty, so they each grabbed a

bowl of chili at the cafeteria and found a seat. After lunch they went up the backside and down a long, meandering green run. After that they tried a black diamond. Dan managed okay, with a few tense turns on the narrow run, but she found it more challenging than enjoyable, her thighs burning and her heart pounding when she reached the bottom. While she enjoyed speed, there was a fine line between in control and out of it, and she didn't often enjoy riding that line. The last thing she wanted to do was have a big crash today.

The sun moved around and Adele took off her goggles in favor of sunglasses. They zoomed down some blue runs, just challenging enough to keep it interesting, and as the light started to dim behind the peaks, they met at the bottom and caught the lift up to the top again.

"Tired?" Dan asked.

"Getting there. Last run, maybe? If you've had enough."

He nodded. "It's been a good day."

It had. They sat in silence for a bit, listening to the whir of the lift, looking down at the trees and snow below them as their feet dangled in the air.

Adele looked over at Dan, marveling that they'd spent a whole day together without talking about the past. She supposed that was because they'd been busy, always moving, with not much time to talk. There'd been a few laughs and some moments to appreciate the scenery.

But the day was drawing to an end, and there was a drive back to Banff and reality staring them in the face.

"Do you want to do that easy run? Might be a nice cooldown before we go."

She nodded. Her legs were starting to feel tired, and all the fresh air and exercise told her she'd sleep well tonight. "That sounds good."

"Ready to put the bar up?"

They lifted the bar as the end of the lift approached. A slight push with her hand had her sliding away from the lift, coming to a stop about twenty feet away, waiting for Dan to come up beside her. Once he did, she smiled and then pushed off with her poles.

The groomed run was a little rougher now after a day of activity. The little bit of fresh snow had been packed down, and there were tiny icy ruts here and there. It presented no problem, but as Adele took lovely sweeping turns, she had the thought that the run was looking as tired as she felt.

A young girl in a pink jacket was up ahead, taking smaller turns and looking a little more uncertain on her skis. Adele went to move to the left to give her lots of room, but two other skiers had come up behind her and were taking the slot, making it impossible for her to move much. No matter. As long as the girl stayed consistent, Adele could slip right by and leave her behind.

She was nearly there, ready to shift her weight onto her left ski for a turn, when the girl wobbled, made a big cut and darted into Adele's path.

Adele pivoted quickly, performing her own sharp turn, but her balance was off, and she executed another sharp turn to the right to avoid other skiers on her left. When she did, the edge of her ski caught a rut and she felt herself going down.

She hit hard, chest and face hitting the packed snow, her skis sprawled out behind her, poles dangling from her wrists by the straps.

"Delly! You okay?"

She pushed herself up on her hands, a bit dazed and winded. She then swiveled her un-

gainly skis around so they were at her side
and she was on her right hip. "I am. Caught
an edge." She looked up into his concerned
face, his skis parked right beside her. "On a
green run. Embarrassing."

"It shouldn't be. That was some pretty im-
pressive evasive action." He chuckled and
moved to her side so he could offer her a hand
to get up.

When she was upright on her skis again,
he frowned. "Del, you're bleeding."

"What?"

He took off his gloves and stuck them between his knees. He then reached for her sunglasses and removed them carefully. "Damn,
Del. You hit your face so hard, the piece on
your glasses cut your nose."

She lifted her hand to her face, and when
she withdrew it again, her mitten had blood
on it. "Oh."

"You feel okay? Dizzy or dazed or anything?"

"Not really. Just…tired. I do think it's time
to go."

"No kidding. Let me put these in your
pocket." He tucked her glasses into her pocket
and zipped it up again. "You sure you're okay
to go down the hill?"

She pushed away his hand. "Of course I am. Don't worry, it's just a minor flesh wound," she joked. She bent to pick up her poles and tried to ignore the heavy feeling behind her eyes. She was going to end up with a headache. Good thing this was the last run.

They made it to the base without incident, but as Adele took off her skis, she had to admit she was feeling a bit off. She'd "had her bell rung" as her grandfather had used to say, and a look at her reflection in a window showed a streak of blood down her nose.

She went to the bathroom while Dan was returning his equipment, and wiped the blood away with a wet paper towel. The fall put a damper on an otherwise lovely day, and she was feeling a bit grumpy because of it.

When she came out again, Dan frowned. "Why don't you let me drive back? You're looking a little pale. You might have given your head a real bump."

She should insist on driving, but instead she unzipped her inside pocket and handed him the keys. "Okay."

Taking off her ski boots and putting on her regular ones was a pain, and she finally buckled her seat belt and leaned back against the headrest. "I normally wouldn't hand over my keys, you know," she said as Dan started the engine. "But I'm tired and that tumble knocked the starch right out of me."

He laughed at her saying and put the car in gear. "It's no big deal, Delly. It was a fun day. You chill. I think we're both going to sleep well tonight."

Forget tonight. The hum of the tires sounded on the highway and Adele decided she'd close her eyes just for a moment.

CHAPTER TEN

DAN LOOKED OVER at Adele, not wanting to wake her. She'd been asleep for nearly twenty minutes and he was actually worried about her having a concussion. They were nearly to the Banff exit, and he didn't know how to get to her house. He was going to have to wake her.

"Adele." When she didn't move, he said a little louder, "Delly." He put his hand on her leg and gave it a little shake.

She came to with several blinks. "Oh," she said softly. "We're almost home."

Home.

Her home, not his, but the simple statement took him back several years to when they'd traveled outside the city to visit his family or go on a day trip. She'd always been one to fall asleep in the car, and he'd awakened her several times in the way he had just now.

"I need directions to your place."

She sat up straighter. "Oh. Just go to the hotel. I can drop you off."

He frowned a little. "Well, I can take a cab from your place. You hit your head pretty hard, and fell asleep as soon as we hit the highway. I'd rather know you're home, safe and sound."

"I don't have a concussion," she said, rolling her neck. "I'm just really tired. But okay. I won't fight you on it. I don't think I'd win, anyway." She sent him a sideways smile and then gave him directions to get to her house.

It was a little thing, set back on a side street, with a cute little sign out front that simply said Hawthorne Weddings. He pulled into the driveway and killed the engine. "I'll help you get your stuff inside."

She nodded and opened the door. "Thanks, Dan."

"Don't thank me." He grinned at her. "I saw you fall. I'm gonna get some mileage out of that graceful endeavor."

The look on her face wiped the smile off his. Of course he wouldn't get mileage out of it. In a few days, he'd be gone, back to his life, leaving her here in hers. A knot formed in his chest at the thought. Now that they'd made peace, he wasn't sure he was comfortable with the idea of never speaking to her ever again. But what was the alternative?

"Forget I said that." He reached up and took her skis off the rack. "I wasn't thinking."

"It's okay. I know what you meant." She smiled back but her eyes seemed sad. "I know I'm not graceful."

"That fall wasn't graceful. I didn't say anything about you, Del."

She shouldered her boot bag and led the way to a side set of steps that led upstairs to her living space. Her entry was a bit crowded, particularly when she stood her skis up on a mat and put her boot bag beside it. "They'll need to dry," she said, shrugging out of her coat. Mr. Num-Nums came rushing around the corner to see her, but halted with a comical look when he saw Dan standing in the doorway. The cat's tail fluffed up with alarm.

"It's okay, buddy," she said quietly. She looked at Dan. "He's a bit shy of strangers."

One of the skis shifted a little and the cat took off. "Sorry."

"Oh, it's fine. He'll come back out in a bit. It just takes him a while to warm up to people. He's much better now than when I first adopted him."

"I'll call a cab. You sure you don't need something for your head? I think you've got a scab forming there already."

She lifted her fingers to her nose and found the little cut already crusting over a bit. "It's not bleeding anymore. And truly, I don't have a headache. I really am just tired. It's all the fresh air."

He nodded and then reached into his pocket for his cell. He didn't want to go. Didn't want the day to end. Didn't know what to say, either, or where they went from here. He'd just brought up a browser to look for a local cab company number when she put her hand on his arm.

"You want some dinner? We just had chili for lunch, and you've been eating hotel food all week. I can make us something."

He met her gaze, wondering what was behind the invitation, wondering if he cared. "I'd like that. But I can help. I'm a decent cook."

"I remember," she said, and the little licks of awareness flickered again. "Come on in. I'll see what's in the freezer."

He followed her inside and immediately felt at home. A flick of a switch turned on a pair of lamps, bathing the room in a cozy glow.

Her sofa and chairs were a warm gold fabric, dotted with deep red and cream-colored throw pillows. The hardwood gleamed, while a coffee table stood on a rug with the same cream, gold and raspberry colors in it. "Have a seat," she called from the kitchen. "Would you like something to drink?" She came back around the corner holding a bottle of red wine in her hand. "Since you're not driving."

"Sure," he replied, but instead of sitting, he followed her into the kitchen. It, too, was cozy, but not cluttered. Cream walls, stainless steel appliances, cupboards in smooth cherry. "I like your place. It suits you."

She smiled as she got out a corkscrew. "Thanks. I painted when I bought the place. I know cream is a little dull, but I can do a lot with it with furniture and decorations. It's like my canvas." She pulled the cork out with a pop. "Particularly if I change my mind about colors. I've actually considered doing something with tan and light blue, kind of an aqua. Or I can leave the walls cream. Airy and light. But I haven't decided yet."

He took the glass she offered and sipped while she opened the freezer at the bottom of her fridge. "How do you feel about beef medallions?"

"I have warm, fuzzy feelings," he admitted, and grinned. For a moment, he'd actually forgotten that she'd trampled his heart.

Her brows came together when she stood up and looked at him, the package of beef in her hands. "What is it? Do you not like the wine?"

It's in the past, he reminded himself. *This is a friendly dinner, nothing more.*

"The wine's great. It's just a little bit strange, is all. Me being here. With you. Sometimes I forget, and then—"

"Sometimes you're reminded," she finished for him. "I know. I've had that feeling all day. And then I remind myself that we're not starting over. We're making peace and letting go. And that's a good thing, Dan. I can't tell you how good it feels to have told you the truth."

He took a long drink of wine. This conversation wasn't a light one, and he felt as if he needed fortification. "I can't say it feels good to me, really," he said honestly. "I mean, I'm trying to not be angry anymore. And I understand a lot. But it's been painful, Delly. I'm not going to pretend it hasn't."

Her face softened. "I know. I'm sorry."

"Would you change the past if you could?"

She swallowed. "I don't know. But it

doesn't matter, because I can't. We can just deal with the present. And right now my present says I'm glad we're not fighting anymore, and it's also saying that in an hour I'm going to be starving, so we should get started on this."

She didn't want to talk about it anymore. He got it; they'd pretty much beaten the subject to death over the last few days. That he had lingering feelings about it was natural, he supposed. Not wanting to retread the same conversation ad nauseam was also natural.

As the meat was defrosting, Adele gave him potatoes to peel, while she mixed up some sort of sauce. Before long, the potatoes were on the stove and the medallions were waiting for the cast-iron pan to heat. Together they built a salad, and then Adele mixed ingredients for a vinaigrette in a bottle.

"Everything from scratch," he remarked.

"Not always, but I do like to cook. And it's nice to cook for someone else, too, and not just me." She grinned. "I've gotten quite good at working with oils and herbs and vegetable combinations. Harper's a vegetarian and comes by usually once a week for dinner."

"The photographer, right?" He remembered her. She had laughing eyes and a bright smile.

She nodded. "Harper's my best friend, really. We met through the business, when I was looking for a local photographer for a wedding. We hit it off and I recommend her quite often now, unless clients have a preference already in mind. She's one of the sweetest, most giving people I know."

He topped up his wine, and hers, too. "That's nice. It's how I feel about Pete, you know?"

"Except you also have brothers and sisters that you're close to. I don't."

He wondered if she ever spoke to her mother, but didn't want to ask. Her upbringing had always been a bit of a sore spot. Her dad had abandoned her mom before Adele was born, and her mom had worked her fingers to the bone to provide for the two of them. As a result, Adele had been on her own a lot as a kid. On her own and lonely.

"True," he said easily, watching her place the medallions in the pan. The hot sizzle of the meat made his stomach growl.

She seared each side and then added sliced mushrooms. She moved around the kitchen with efficiency and confidence. After draining the potatoes, she put the balsamic glaze she'd mixed up into the pan, and while it began to reduce, she whipped the potatoes and piped them through a bag onto a baking sheet. "You're getting fancy on me," he said, intrigued.

"I love Duchess potatoes," she admitted, sliding the pan into the oven. "Crispy on the outside, but creamy and delicious on the inside. It won't be long now."

She got out plates and cutlery and handed them to him, along with a couple of placemats. "You can set the table."

"Yes, boss." He gave a mock salute and grinned. She'd always had confidence, but now it was different. It was backed up by a self-assurance, a maturity he liked. A lot. She'd been the same way at the wedding, even when things had gone wrong. As if she'd handled tough days before and knew she could do so again.

When they sat down to eat, Dan knew he couldn't have found a better meal anywhere in town. Two perfect spirals of potatoes were on his plate, along with rich glazed medallions and the colorful salad. It smelled amazing.

"Thank you for this," he said, raising his glass. "To a good day. No, scratch that. A great day."

"Except for me falling on my face," she added drily, but touched the rim of her glass to his anyway.

He laughed. "Well, yes. Except for that. How're you feeling?"

She shrugged and took a bite of potato. "Oh, more embarrassed than anything."

"You would have felt worse if you'd plowed over that girl," he remarked. He cut into the beef. Cooked perfectly, with a lovely stripe of pink in the middle. The first bite was heaven.

"This is amazing."

"Thank you." She blushed a little, he noticed, and then she looked down at her plate.

"I mean it, Delly. This is delicious. And so much better than eating alone at the hotel."

She looked up at him. "That's not the first time you've mentioned being alone. Are you lonely, Dan?"

He tried not to choke, and swallowed a piece of beef that was perhaps a little too big. He reached for his glass and took a hearty drink of wine. He then looked up at her. She was waiting for him to answer, her empty fork poised in midair.

"I'm usually too busy to be lonely," he admitted. "I have long hours at the office. This week I find myself at loose ends more often than not. I'm just not used to it."

"Depends," she mused, spearing a piece of cucumber.

"Depends on what?"

"On if you're too busy so you don't have to be lonely. If it's a distraction."

He stared at her.

"Speaking from experience, here. Sometimes it's hard to be alone with yourself. So you fill up the hours with stuff to avoid it."

"Delly, I…no. I just have a demanding job."

"Okay. I just thought I'd ask. I have a lot of experience with this sort of thing."

His appetite suddenly wasn't as keen. Was she partly right? It was ridiculous, wasn't it? He was CFO of a major company, the youngest member of the C-suite. He'd had to work long hours to get where he was and he didn't regret it.

But had it been a convenient way to keep from being lonely? To fill his time so he didn't have time to think too much?

"I hit a nerve. I'm sorry."

Her voice was soft and reminded him of too many dinners they'd shared, sitting across from each other at a small table in his apartment, or hers. "It's okay. To be honest, I've spent the last four years working my butt off to get where I am in the company. I'm the youngest executive. It required a few sacrifices. Personal time being one of them."

Of course, it had kept him from forming deep, personal connections. He'd only dated a handful of women, and then it had been five, maybe six dates and they went their own way. Anytime he'd sensed things getting a little too close, he'd backed off. He liked keeping it uncomplicated. He moved on before... well... Before a woman had a chance of actually getting him to care too much. He was the one who did the leaving, not the other way around.

And before she had time to get too attached.

The potatoes were suddenly dry in his mouth. Did he really do that?

He looked over at Adele, who was watching him with her eyes wide and filled with curiosity. "Where'd you go?" she asked, frowning a little. "You got very quiet all of a sudden."

He wasn't sure what to say. They'd had a nice day, but spilling his guts to his ex didn't seem like a smart move. Particularly since he suspected his thoughts were somehow tangled up in her leaving him in the first place.

"I don't know," he replied, cutting into his steak again to avoid meeting her gaze. "Just thinking you might be right about the all-work-and-no-play thing."

She chuckled then, lightening the mood a bit. "And you were on my case for never playing hooky. When was the last time you did?"

He looked up and offered a wry smile. "A planned vacation is as close as it gets. And this is my first one in nearly two years."

"Then I'm glad you didn't leave last night and you're taking a few more days."

"Me too."

They finished their meal and he helped load the plates into the dishwasher. Then he dried when she washed the pots and pans by hand. It only took a few moments, and he knew he should leave, but he wasn't ready to go back to an empty hotel room with nothing but the TV for company. When she reached for the wine bottle and refilled their glasses, he didn't protest. Instead he took his and followed her into the living room.

"Are you cold?" she asked.

She was still wearing the leggings and sweater from skiing, and he'd changed back into jeans when he'd returned the skis at the hill. The room was warm but not overly so, but he suspected she was chilly, so he answered, "If you're thinking of turning on the fireplace, that might be nice."

All it took was the press of a button and the gas fireplace came to life with a *poof.* The lamps and the flickering fire lent the room a soft glow, and they sat on either end of the sofa. Adele let out a long sigh, the soft sound reaching inside him and making him wish things he had no right wishing. This was Adele. Delly. They were over. He had no right to be thinking of her in *that* way.

Except he was. Because he'd never been as comfortable with anyone as he was with her. Even now, with that little bit of awkwardness between them, there was something else, something bigger, making him feel as though this was where he was meant to be.

"This is nice," she said quietly, her head back against the cushion but turned in his direction. "I'm going to be sore tomorrow, but the whole day was so fun. Thank you for convincing me to take it off."

"You're welcome. Everyone needs a little R & R."

"Even big-shot CFOs?" she asked, a smile playing on her lips.

"Even them," he admitted, though he didn't

want to examine his own motives too closely. He wasn't sure he'd like what he would find.

He lifted his right foot and tucked it under his left leg so he was sitting slightly sideways on the sofa. Adele was taking a drink of her wine and he watched her, the way her lips touched the rim of the glass, how the lamp-light shone off her hair, the graceful arch of her throat as she swallowed the wine. It took him back once again to the "old days," when they'd stay in on a Friday or Saturday night and simply chill out.

She turned her head and looked at him, and his heart stuttered. "I missed this, Delly," he whispered. "I missed you."

Alarm widened her eyes for a moment, quickly replaced with regret. "I'm sorry," she answered. "I don't... I can't... Things are all jumbled up. I don't know how to respond to that."

"I know." He put his wine down on the cof-fee table and slid a little closer, close enough that he could reach out and take her hand. "Tonight, cooking with you, eating with you, sitting here...it feels like it used to feel, you know? And that's something I haven't had since you left."

Her fingers tightened on his, and his chest

started to cramp. What was he doing? He had to be crazy. But since the first moment he'd seen her again, back at the hotel, he'd been unable to stop thinking about her. First in anger, then in surprise, and now because he wanted to kiss her and he knew it would be a horrible mistake. They couldn't erase the past or the years since.

"I feel the same way," she whispered. "When I saw you at the hotel that first day, it was like my whole world came crashing down. I thought I'd done such a great job building a life without you, and then there you were and I realized I hadn't done that great a job at all. Added to that was my guilt and regret. I can't begin to tell you how much it means to me that we're speaking. That you listened."

Speaking. Listened. She was talking about closure, wasn't she? And he had been, too, until about an hour ago. Being in her home changed things. It was so personal, so intimate. Homes were a reflection of the person within. Hers was warm and welcoming. When he thought about his own apartment, he realized it was more...functional. A dwelling, but not really a home.

Delly was also warm and welcoming.

Whereas Dan was simply going through the motions.

But not here. Not with her. He was feeling more alive than he had in months, and he didn't want it to end. He was tired of going through the motions.

"Dan," she said, a note of caution in her voice, but a note of something else, too.

He reached for her glass and took it from her hands, putting it on the coffee table beside his own glass. As he leaned back, he slid over closer to her, so only a few inches separated them on the cushions.

His gaze met hers. His heart was pounding, oh, so hard as he looked into her face. Today had been so perfect. They'd laughed and talked, and being with her had been so easy. It still was. He lifted his hand and put his fingers gently along the side of her neck, felt her pulse beneath the tips. Then he did what he'd promised himself he wouldn't: he leaned in and kissed her.

CHAPTER ELEVEN

SHE COULDN'T BREATHE.

Adele sat perfectly still on her sofa, trying hard not to melt into his touch, although she wanted to. So badly. Dan, in her house, on her sofa, his lips softly touching hers, as if asking permission. It was remarkably sweet and hurt her heart just a bit when she thought of all they'd been through.

"Del," he murmured, his fingers sliding off her neck and onto her shoulder, where he squeezed just a little bit.

His lips tasted sharp and rich, like the wine they'd been drinking, and she couldn't hold her breath any longer. Instead she let out a sigh, inhaled, and met his mouth equally with her own, lifting her arms around his neck.

Once she acquiesced, everything changed.

The first touch of their mouths had been a question, but this—oh, this was the answer.

Nothing was fevered or panicked; instead, it was a slow burn, a gentle sinking into it that was heavenly. The feel of him, the taste…it was all so familiar, and yet exciting, too. He was the same man and yet not. Just as she was not the same woman.

He ran his fingers through her hair, sliding them into the soft strands with a tenderness that blew her away. She knew what awaited her if they took this further. Knew how he'd touch her, how he'd sound, what he'd feel like in the dark. A part of her craved that feeling again, but another part was wise enough to know it would be a mistake. A big one. She kept her eyes closed and gave herself another few moments to enjoy the sensation before breaking off the kiss and sitting back a little.

"Some things haven't changed," he breathed, his hand dropping to rest on her knee.

"But too much has changed for us to think we can turn back the clock." She lifted her eyes and nearly melted at the soft, stunned look in his. He hadn't expected it to be so good either, had he? "Yesterday you were furious with me. Now… I don't know what to say right now," she admitted.

"Don't say anything. Let's not ruin it,

okay?" It was as if they were both worried that they'd say the wrong word and the fragile link between them would shatter like glass. "It's time for me to go. I'll go call the cab."

She nodded mutely, not trusting herself to reply. The words "not yet" sat on her tongue, but she knew it would be wrong to say them. It was better he leave now. Better that she regain her balance and have time to think about what had happened today. The kiss was only part of it. She was smart enough to know that their relationship, if they could call it that, had shifted.

And that with the barriers dropped, she'd caught glimpses of the Dan she remembered, and had loved.

Now they'd kissed. Kissed! Were they crazy? It was definitely time to step back.

He came back into the living room, putting his phone back in his pocket. "About ten minutes, they said."

She got up from the sofa before he had a chance to sit down again. "Do you have all your stuff?"

He laughed and lifted the small day pack he'd brought. "The running leggings I wore under my ski pants. That's it."

Right. He'd rented everything else. "Oh. Well. Do you want leftovers?"

She started to move to the kitchen and he reached out and put his hand on her arm. "What would I do with them? I'm staying in a hotel room," he reminded her softly. "I know you're flustered. It's okay. Take a breath."

She did, and it didn't help. But she pretended it did, and moved away from his touch, leading the way to the entrance. "Right. Of course you are. I'm sorry."

"Don't apologize. It took us both by surprise."

She would have answered him back, something about it not happening again, when headlights flashed through the front windows. Forget ten minutes; the cab had only taken maybe three. She watched as he pulled on his boots and snagged his ski pants from a hook.

"Thank you. For a wonderful day and a delicious dinner."

"You're welcome."

He hesitated and her breath caught in her throat as he hovered, as if unsure of what to do next. He leaned forward and placed a light kiss on her lips, leaving her stunned.

"See you soon, Delly," he murmured, and then went out the door, closing it behind him.

She leaned back against the wall, her fingers pressed to her lips. Not "goodbye," but "see you soon."

They couldn't start anything up again. They couldn't.

But they already had. And she had no idea what to do about it.

The next morning she met Harper at her studio, a rented space on one of the town's side streets. The storefront showcased some of Harper's non-portrait work, and when Adele stepped inside, Harper's assistant greeted her.

"Hi, Juny." Adele smiled at the young woman. "Is Harper in the back?"

"She is. Wait'll you see what she's got." Juny's smile was wide. Today her hair was pulled back in a messy bun, the purple streaks adding a splash of color and revealing the small tattoo behind her ear. Juny was smart, friendly and delightfully quirky. At twenty-one, she often made Adele wonder if Harper had been the same at that age.

Intrigued by the "what she's got" mention, Adele stepped into the back of the shop to the studio. There was a large section that Harper used for indoor portrait sittings, and another for her equipment and computer, and finally a small dark room where she did her own developing.

"Harper? You back here?"

"Hang on! In the bathroom!" came the call.

Adele wandered through the room for a few minutes, pausing to look at some of the photographs sitting on a side table. These weren't Harper's wedding photos; the stack held a variety of outdoor shots, some with snow, some not, as well as some close-ups and panoramic landscapes. All of them were stunning, in Adele's eyes. Her friend had a big talent.

The door to the bathroom opened and Harper came out, a huge grin on her face. "I'm so glad you're here! Sorry I wasn't out right away. I brought in pastries and my fingers were full of glaze."

"It's okay. I was browsing." She pointed to the stack.

Harper frowned. "Sweetie, that's my reject pile."

"Shut up," Adele replied. "They're gorgeous."

"Thank you for saying so." Harper came closer and slid into her desk chair. "Pull up a pew. I want to show you some shots I took last weekend."

"Awesome. I was feeling so cruddy, I hardly

remember parts of it. I take it they turned out well?"

Harper scrolled through thumbnails until she found the one she wanted and popped it up on the screen, full-size. "Hunka, hunka burnin' love," she said, her voice low.

It was a picture of Dan, dressed in dark jeans and a sweater, the night of the rehearsal. He had one hand in his pocket and was laughing at something Pete was saying. Adele got that strange feeling of lightness in her stomach just looking at it.

"That's nice, but what about the wedding shots?"

"Oh, we'll get to those." She brought up another, which was a candid shot of Adele and Dan by the chairs. Adele was threading navy satin through the rungs, and Dan was holding another swath of fabric in his hands.

"Seriously," Adele chided, the butterflies growing. "Did you take any pictures of the bride and groom?"

Harper laughed and looked up at her. "Oh, hundreds. Hang on. There's another few I want you to see."

The few included one of them loading the ice sculptures together, followed by one where Adele was off to the side, speaking to a bridesmaid and smiling, while Dan looked on.

It wasn't anything spectacular, until she looked at Dan's face.

Harper knew the moment she got it, because she said, "That is not the face of a man who doesn't care. Damn, girl. That's *longing* right there."

Heat rushed into Adele's cheeks. "Don't be silly."

"You're blushing. What's going on?" She pushed her chair back. "Have you seen him again?"

Adele didn't answer, but she had never had a good poker face. "You have," Harper said, leaning back in her chair. "Stay here. I'm going to make tea. And you're going to tell me everything."

While Harper went to the corner of the room that held a microwave, bar fridge and kettle, Adele stared at the picture on the monitor and wondered what Harper would say if she knew the truth.

Since telling Dan, she'd felt so much lighter. Without this deep, dark secret following her around. She couldn't imagine Harper being judgy about it. But she might offer a little bit of perspective where Dan was concerned. It wasn't as simple as rekindling something, no matter what the photo seemed to imply. It was complicated, and the biggest issue of all wasn't fixable.

Harper came back with a steaming mug of mint tea and put it in front of Adele. "You look like your brain hurts," Harper commented, sitting back in her chair. "What's going on?"

Adele blew on her tea. "So, I did see Dan the other day. He asked me to lunch to apologize."

"After the fruit basket?"

"Yeah."

"It didn't go well, I take it."

She sipped the tea. The mint was fresh and calming—just what she needed. "It started off okay. But ended with a big argument and talking about how our relationship ended." She took a big breath and met Harper's gaze. "I finally told him why I left. It was…difficult."

Harper was quiet for a moment. "I take it this is more than I already know."

Adele nodded. "More than I've ever said out loud to anyone. And I'm glad we talked. It was one of the hardest afternoons I've had since…well, since we broke up." And that was saying something. There'd been plenty of difficult afternoons during her illness.

Silence fell for a few minutes and then Harper put her hand over Adele's. "I can tell this is something really hard for you. You don't have to share if you don't want to. I know there are some things that are too painful to put into words."

Adele wondered what she meant, or how she knew, but it did make her feel better. Safe. She looked into her best friend's eyes and saw compassion and acceptance. And also strength. She nodded and said the words for the second time that week.

"I can't have children. I had cancer."

Harper's eyes softened and she gave a small nod. "I see. I'm sorry, honey."

"It's okay. I had cervical cancer and they had to take my uterus. Then I had radiation."

"God." Harper reached over and took Adele's free hand. "This was when you were twenty-one?"

"Yeah. Nearly twenty-two."

"And you were alone."

Harper already knew about Adele's difficult relationship with her mother. Adele hadn't seen her in three years now. "Pretty much," Adele admitted.

"And this is why you broke up with Dan?"

She nodded, and proceeded to explain her rationale, with Harper sipping her tea and nodding occasionally. But when she got to the part about why she'd avoided telling Dan the real reason why, a frown appeared in the form of a wrinkle at the top of Harper's nose.

"I don't understand," she said, putting down her cup. "Why not explore other options? Like adoption? Why was it all or nothing?"

Adele sighed. "This is where my logic seemed so right at the time but isn't as clear-cut right now. I knew he'd say it would be okay and we'd work through it together, but I felt like he'd feel he had to say that no matter what he really thought. That I'd be tempted to stay and then he'd end up resenting me, or we'd grow apart and I'd be even more broken."

"So you ran away instead."

"Something like that. Adoption isn't easy. And I was honestly stuck on the fact that I wouldn't be able to provide him with his own child."

"And is that important? The blood connection?"

Adele looked at Harper. "Not as much now as it had seemed then, if I'm honest. I made the decision in a time of stress and confusion, you know? I felt like…such a failure. And since then, I kept telling myself he was probably happy with someone else. Someone with a whole reproductive system." She gave a short laugh. "Look, I know it sounds awful now. My logical brain tells me that it doesn't matter if I have a uterus. I'm a woman without it. My emotional brain…not so much. And back then I was running on emotion. All the time."

Harper nodded. "Of course you were. But he's not happy with someone else, is he?"

Adele shook her head. "Apparently not. We…we spent yesterday together. Went skiing. Had dinner." She paused. "At my place."

Harper gave a shove with her feet so that her rolling chair came to a few inches of Adele's knees. "Did he stay over?"

Adele laughed. "You sound far too excited about that prospect. No. But we had a very nice day. And some wine. And he…he kissed me."

"Holy." Harper put her hands on the arms of Adele's chair. "So, are you starting something up again? Getting back together?"

Why was excitement rising up in her chest? Adele pushed it back, trying to be rational. "No, don't be silly. We got caught up in a moment, that's all. I mean…" She searched for rational thought. "He's leaving at the end of the week. He lives in Toronto and my business is here. This is just…closure."

"Kissing doesn't seem like closure to me."

"It is, though. It has to be. It's just…working through old feelings we didn't get a chance to work through before."

"If you say so." Harper swiveled and pointed to the picture on the screen. "This does not look like a man who has left the past behind."

But he had to. They didn't have a future. Too much had happened. And nothing had really changed. She couldn't wave a magic wand and be able to bear children. And adoption… not everyone wanted to go that route. It also wasn't as easy as deciding to do it and *poof*, a baby showed up.

The one thing that kept getting her stuck was that the facts didn't reconcile with her feelings. Tears pricked her eyes and she was mortified.

"Oh, honey." Harper touched her hand. "Do you still love him?"

"I don't know," she said, her voice a soft wail. "Oh, Harper. I'm so stupid. I can't still love him. Seriously, I think it's just dealing with things that should have been dealt with years ago."

"Except…"

"Except it doesn't feel like that. Yesterday, when we were together…it felt so right. So familiar. I don't want to fall into the *familiar* trap or the *get it right the next time* trap. And it would be so easy. He's so…"

"He's so what?"

She didn't answer out loud, but in her head she heard the word. *Everything.*

Harper sighed. "Drink your tea. You want to come to my place for dinner tonight? Get some perspective? I'm making chickpea curry."

Normally Adele would grab at the chance. Harper was a beautiful cook, and Adele had learned to eat a lot of vegetarian food in her kitchen. Curry was one of Harper's specialties. "Not tonight. I need to do some thinking."

"All right. And, Adele, thanks for sharing that with me. I feel privileged."

"You're the best friend I have. I trust you."

"I trust you, too. Now, do you want to see the rest of the wedding pictures?"

"I'd love to." Adele leaned forward and cradled her now lukewarm tea, feeling more at peace than she had in a long time.

Maybe it was time she started trusting people again.

CHAPTER TWELVE

DAN STARED AT the ceiling in his hotel room. He only had three days left in Banff and then he was supposed to be in Calgary. Yesterday—Thursday—was the only day he hadn't seen Adele other than the Monday following the wedding, when she'd still been sick. He'd thought he needed space after that kiss. Instead he'd spent the whole day preoccupied, despite taking a trip up the gondola and then a soak in the hot springs to ease his ski legs. It had been incredibly lonely, doing those things by himself.

Which was odd. Whenever he traveled for work, he enjoyed taking in some of the sights of his destination. Seeing Delly again had changed everything.

And thinking about it, like he was doing now, was solving nothing.

It had been a shock, hearing that she couldn't

have children, and now that it had all sunk in, he kept asking himself if it would have made a difference back then. He knew without a doubt that he would have stood by her, but she wasn't wrong when she said he'd always wanted a family of his own.

He still did. But he also thought that if given the choice, he wouldn't forsake a woman he loved just because she couldn't bear children through no fault of her own.

His aunt had had breast cancer and a double mastectomy. He remembered her saying once to his mother that she felt like less of a woman right after the surgery. He wondered if Adele had felt that way, too. But when he looked at her, he didn't see someone with parts missing, or anything "less than." Instead he saw a strong, brave woman. A survivor.

He just hoped she saw herself the same way.

When he'd had enough of pondering while staring at the ceiling, he rolled out of bed and padded over to the TV stand, where he'd left his phone to charge. He unplugged it and pressed the button. His email notification icon was up on the top left, as well as a little envelope. A text message.

He ignored the email and hit the text.

Morning. Feel like doing something today?

His heart took a leap. They couldn't start something back up again. It would be foolish. But he wanted to see her.

He typed back.

What do you have in mind?

Her answer came soon.

Dogsledding in Canmore.

It was not what he'd expected.

I've never done that before.

Then you're in for a treat. Pick you up at one.

He had four hours to kill before she arrived, so he had a shower, ordered up some breakfast, and scrolled through his email and newsfeed. He also answered a few questions from the Calgary office he was looking forward to visiting on Monday.

With offices now in Edmonton and Calgary, and a proposed one in British Columbia, the regional business was growing and it was exciting to see. As much as he'd worked hard to climb the corporate ladder in Toronto, what really got him excited was expansion. The world was changing, and business had to change with it. He was more than just the numbers guy.

He found Adele in the lobby, waiting for him just before one o'clock, and he saw her before she had a chance to see him. She was speaking to one of the doormen, and he took a moment to stare. She was dressed for the weather—leggings with warm boots, her puffy jacket, and a band that went around her head and covered her ears, while still allowing her hair to flow down over her collar. Pink seemed to be her color, as her headband and scarf were a pastel shade, like the blooms on his mother's rose bush when they were wide open. He had really missed her over the years, more than he realized. Oh, at first it had been horrible. His heart had been thoroughly broken, and there was no sense denying it. But seeing her now made him wonder if this was what had been missing from his life all along.

And that was a dangerous thought. Wasn't this going down a road that led nowhere?

She turned around and saw him there and a

smile bloomed across her face. He smiled in return and knew he was in deep, deep trouble.

And yet, even knowing it didn't stop him from dropping a light kiss on her lips as he joined her.

"Hi," he said softly, smiling down at her. The fact that her eyes were slightly dazed after the simple kiss didn't escape him.

"Hi yourself. That was…unexpected."

"For me, too," he admitted. "It just felt… right."

Her cheeks colored and she turned away. "Come on. We're on for one thirty."

"Are we cutting it close?" He fell into step beside her as she started toward the front door.

"We've got time. They'll walk us through stuff for a half hour first, then an hour on the trail, and then snacks and stuff after. I wasn't sure you'd want a longer ride today."

"No, that sounds perfect." They'd be done by three thirty, back in Banff at four and have the rest of the day to…well, do something. If they wanted.

She turned into a lane marked with a sign for Three Sisters Dogsledding. It ran for nearly a kilometer, bordered by fragrant evergreens until it ended near a large house at one side and then a long building that housed the equipment and kennel facilities. They could hear the barking before they even got out of the car, and Adele flashed him a happy grin. "This is cool," he remarked, grinning back. "I've never done this before."

"I have. Once," she revealed, turning off the car. "We did a wedding nearby last year. It was probably the most unusual ceremony I've ever planned. All the guests were taken by sled to the location, and the bride and groom came last. It made for fantastic photos. Cold, but fantastic."

She got out of the car and reached in the back for the rest of her winter gear. "I booked us with a driver," she called as he got out of the car. "I've driven before, briefly, but I thought this would be more relaxing."

He looked over toward a nearby sled. It had a cover that zipped up, so the passengers would be cozy inside. The idea of her being snuggled up so closely to him made his blood heat.

"Adele! So good to see you again!" A man, probably in his midthirties, strode toward them, dressed in a heavy jacket and a hat with a huge tassel on the end.

"Hey, Jerry. You too." She reached out and

shook his hand. "This is my friend Dan. He's never done this before, so it's gonna be fun. Dan, Jerry was my go-to for everything to do with the wedding last year."

Dan took a moment or two to size up this Jerry guy. He wasn't exactly jealous, but he was aware of the casual familiarity between Jerry and Adele, as well as the smile on the other man's face. He was big, and not a bad-looking sort. Not that Dan had any claim to Adele at all. But still.

"Welcome, Dan. It's a beautiful day, so you're in for a treat. It's a ten-kilometer ride today, over the pond and with beautiful views. Did you bring a camera?"

"I did, though it's just a point and shoot."

"Hard to take a bad one," Jerry said easily. "Come on in, and we'll do the orientation."

Over the next thirty minutes, he learned about the dogs and the basics of sledding, but he only listened with half an ear. The other half was tuned to Delly, the way she smiled and how she laughed when she got licked in the face by one of the dogs. She looked over at him, one hand on the heavy gray fur, and he knew he was in dangerous territory. It would be so easy to fall for her again. And yet a mistake, too. It wasn't even so much that she couldn't have children. It was more that she hadn't trusted him with it. That she'd lied. And even knowing the reason—even understanding—didn't change the feeling that he couldn't trust her, either.

And that was no way to build a relationship. Or rebuild, as the case may be. Even if he wanted to.

"You're looking awfully serious," Delly said, coming to his side. "You okay?"

"Just thinking," he answered, chasing away the thoughts. "Do you think we'll be warm enough?"

She nodded. "We'll be snug as a bug. You'll see."

Jerry waved them out to where their sled awaited. Adele got in and Dan sat in behind her, his legs on either side of hers, like they'd be if they were on a toboggan. Jerry handed them a wool blanket, and then zipped the sled bag around them, covering their legs and middles, and protecting them from wind. The dogs were harnessed, barking and prancing excitedly, ready to go. As Jerry stood on the runners at the back and gripped the handle, Delly turned her head to look at Dan. Her eyes sparkled in the winter sun, her smile radiant. "You ready?"

"So ready," he said, and felt himself slide a little further into...well, surely not love, but something deeper than a simple reconciliation. Not closure, but...a new beginning somehow. Despite all his best warnings, something was happening here that he was helpless to stop.

They took off, the sled skimming over the snow, moving faster and faster as they left the yard behind and moved out onto the open trail. Delly laughed, the feeling rumbling against his chest, even through their heavy coats. He smiled, wrapping his arms around her, not caring about holding himself back from her right now. He liked being with her. He liked her laugh and her smile and the sound of her voice, the way she felt in his arms and the vanilla scent of her hair from beneath her headband.

Different than he remembered, but somehow the same, too.

The scenery was stunning as they skimmed over the snow, past trees and bushes and out into an open space, a frozen pond that opened up to the most stunning vista he'd ever seen. Jagged gray peaks topped with pristine snow, naked above the tree line, and in sharp relief to the piercing blue sky. The wind buffeted his cheeks, stinging a bit, but he didn't mind. It was a weird and neat feeling, being so low to the ground, rushing over the snow with a near-weightless sensation.

Delly's arms came over top of his, holding him close against her, and for a moment he dropped his forehead to the back of her head. This was a near-perfect moment, and he let it soak in.

After nearly half an hour, they stopped and got out to stretch their legs and give the dogs a quick break. As Delly stopped and scratched the belly of one, he knelt beside her and rubbed the dog's head. The dog, loving the attention, wriggled around on his back with pleasure.

"You like dogs," he observed.

"Of course I do. But I'm gone so much for work that I can't see having one. Unless I hired a dog walker. Some days, though, I leave the house at seven and don't get home until midnight. Particularly wedding days. It's just not fair."

"So you have Mr. Num-Nums."

She scratched behind the dog's ears. "I do. And he's the best."

He laughed and then decided to get out his camera. He took several shots of the surrounding Rockies, a bunch of the dogs and even Jerry. Then there were snaps of Delly— patting the dogs, making a snow angel, looking back over her shoulder at him.

She was so easy to love. Like she had been back before her diagnosis. Open and artless. It was why he'd thought she'd found someone else. She'd stopped sharing. Now he knew why.

Jerry offered to take a picture of the two of them together, so he handed over the camera and they took a couple of pictures: one kneeling down with a couple of the blue-eyed dogs, and another with the mountains behind them. By then it was time to get back in the sled and head back to base.

Delly felt chilled, so he cuddled her close inside the sled bag. When they reached the main yard, Jerry sent them off with good wishes and told them to enjoy the fire and refreshments.

There was hot cider and cinnamon buns waiting for them, and they sat around the fire and enjoyed. But something else was rising between them now, too. Not a goodbye, like the other night might have been. But a new start. Not just forgiveness, but a moving forward. The two of them, together.

It was time he faced the fact that he'd never gotten over her. And the new revelation that he didn't want to.

Considering he only had a few more days left of his vacation, it meant he only had about forty-eight hours to convince her they were worth fighting for.

There wasn't a moment to lose.

Adele couldn't stop the butterflies in her stomach. They'd been there from the moment Dan had curled his strong arms around her in the sled and hadn't let up, even though their afternoon was done. They'd finished the ride, thoroughly exhilarated, and she'd felt him watching her as they drank mulled cider and munched on sweets. Now, though, it was time to go home. The afternoon was over. And she was wondering what was next. If there was anything. Was she misreading his signals? Were they a product of her own wishful thinking?

They were almost to her car when he came around to the driver's side and took her hand. "Delly, have dinner with me. This has been too great a day for it to end already."

Her heart warmed at his words. "Really?"

"Really." His body was close to hers, close

enough she had to tilt her head up to meet his gaze. "Let's have a real dinner, something special. Not a quick sandwich or an après-ski at your house. Something decadent and…"

Her throat tightened with nerves as she asked, "Are you talking about a date, Dan?"

His hand covered hers on the door handle of her car. "Yes, I am. A date. Does that mean you're going to say no?"

She should. She should tell him with no ambiguity that they absolutely could not go on a date. But then, what was this afternoon if not a date? Just because it was outside didn't make it an un-date.

When she didn't answer right away, he squeezed her fingers. "Go home, get dressed up. We can do this right."

"Dan, I—"

"Don't say no. It's Friday. I leave Sunday night. We have so little time. Let me treat you to dinner, with candles and wine and music and just…"

"And just what?" Her heart pounded, afraid of what he was suggesting, wanting it more than was wise. If they both knew that he was leaving in two days, no one would get the wrong idea, would they? Couldn't they enjoy these few moments? Hadn't they earned it?

"I don't know. I don't have any expectations. I'm not looking further ahead than tonight, okay? I'm asking for one simple date, with no weddings to fret over or secrets to reveal. Just you and me."

"Okay." She answered quickly, surprising herself.

"Really?"

She nodded. "Yes. I'll drop you off, go home and change, and meet you…wherever. Text me the location and I'll be there."

Her eyes met his. She was surprised at the fire flickering in the brown depths.

"Good." He pulled his fingers from hers. "Then let's get going."

She unlocked the car and got inside, nerves still jumbling around as he got in beside her and whipped out his phone. She smiled to herself as they headed back toward Banff, the highway clear and traffic moderate during the weekend rush hour. Her face felt hot to the touch; she wasn't sure if she was blushing or if the wind had chapped her cheeks. Regardless, anticipation curled inside her as she wondered what the night would bring.

The drive seemed to take no time at all and she dropped him back at the hotel. By the time she got home, got inside and fed Mr.

Num-Nums, she had the text with the restaurant name and time. He'd been able to get a seven o'clock reservation and they were going to eat fondue at a neighboring resort.

She smiled to herself. While she'd organized dinners at this location, she'd never actually eaten there herself, though she'd wanted to. It was bound to be a leisurely meal, nestled away near the river and the golf course, private and romantic. She jumped in the shower and scrubbed away the dog smell and the hat hair, and then let her hair air-dry as she picked out her dress and started her makeup.

At six forty-five a taxi pulled up outside and she buttoned up her coat and wondered, for the millionth time, if she should have worn shoes instead of boots. But she loved her knee boots with the skinny heels, and thought they suited the black sweater dress that hugged her curves and had a deep scoop neckline that hinted at the tiniest bit of cleavage. A long necklace took away the bareness, and she'd decided to put her hair up in a messy arrangement that she hoped looked sexy and rumpled. She'd gone for a dramatic eye with painstakingly applied liner, but an understated lip.

She'd dressed for a date—something she hadn't done for many, many months. And never with quite as much care as tonight.

Because Dan mattered. More than she wanted to admit, but there it was.

He was waiting for her at the restaurant, standing just inside, and she caught her breath.

She wasn't the only one who'd dressed for the date. He wore a charcoal-gray suit, perfectly fitted, with a black dress shirt and no tie. She loved that little detail about him— that he kept that top-shirt button carelessly undone. It left the hollow of his neck exposed and she wondered if she'd have the opportunity to kiss it later.

"You look beautiful," he said quietly, reaching for her coat.

"So do you," she replied, and decided it was true. He was beautiful. Who said that word had to be reserved for females only?

They were led to their table. She wondered if he'd somehow managed to sweet-talk them into a corner table because the room was fairly full.

He waited until she was seated, and then took his chair. The room had low lighting, with flickering tea candles adding ambience to each table. They were provided with a menu and asked for a drink order.

"White?" Dan asked. "To start?"

She nodded. "Maybe a Riesling would be lovely."

When the waiter was gone, she let her gaze touch Dan's. "This is so nice. I've never eaten here. Always wanted to, though. It's a favorite for pre-wedding dinners."

He smiled. "I'm glad. This is your home turf, and I wanted tonight to be special."

"It is…whether I'd been here before or not."

The waiter came back with their wine and poured a little in her glass for her to taste. The smooth, slightly tart flavor was perfect, and she nodded and put her glass back down so he could fill it.

"Do you want to do the dinner with pairings?" Dan asked. "It has cheese and chocolate fondue with a schnitzel course in between."

"That sounds amazing."

They handed back their menus, and when the waiter was gone, Dan raised his glass.

"Cheers," he said simply, touching the rim of his glass to hers. She was glad there was no big toast tonight. She wanted to keep it simple.

"This is delicious. And could be a bit dangerous with pairings. I'll have to pace myself."

He smiled at her, his eyes twinkling. "You could always stay over with me."

She simply stared, unsure of what to say, startled by the sudden increase of sexual tension between them. He chuckled, sending her a wink. "Don't panic. I can sleep on the sofa again."

She held his gaze for a moment, and then said softly, "I'm not sure you'd have to."

The twinkle faded from his eyes, replaced by a smoldering fire that said she wasn't alone in her feelings. She did want to be with him again. The kiss the other night had started it, but today, being held close in his arms in the sled…it had felt so right.

"Are we starting something here, Delly? And I don't mean a fling for a few days, but really starting something. Do you want to try again?"

Her chest cramped at the sincerity in his words. It wasn't just the attraction that hadn't gone away. She cared for him so much. Always had. He might have hated her for a while, but she hadn't really stopped loving him. She'd let him go *because* she'd loved him, not because she'd stopped. And maybe they needed to talk about *that*.

Their starter salads were discreetly delivered, and yet neither of them picked up their forks. Instead Dan waited for her answer, and she tried to figure out how to phrase what she needed to say.

"Dan, I…" She pursed her lips, but then decided to just be honest and let the words come. "I never left you because I'd stopped caring about you. The only thing that kept me from running back to you was the thought that I'd done you a favor by setting you free. It seemed so unfair to make you a victim to…to my illness. But it was never because I didn't love you. And I'm starting to think that maybe I never really stopped."

Other diners chatted and ate all around them, with the tinkling of silverware and porcelain and murmured voices. But Adele felt as if she and Dan were in their own little bubble where time stood still for just a few moments as he absorbed her words.

He reached across the table and took her fingers in his. "You broke my heart," he admitted softly. "And you broke my trust, Delly. But I never really got over you, either."

The cramp was still centered in her chest,

a confusing combination of anticipation and fear. Where would all this lead? Was she ready for it? Was he? Because nothing had changed. Not really.

"I can see your mind working," he said, laughing a little and dispelling a bit of the tension. "We don't have to have all the answers now, Del. Let's leave it at you care about me, and I care about you, and we'll take this one day at a time. One hour at a time, if we need to."

It was good advice. It was the kind of advice she'd been given during her treatment. But could she really let go of her reservations and just *be* with him? Was that realistic, considering the circumstances? She wanted it to be, and maybe that was enough.

"That sounds good," she murmured, picking up her fork. "In the moment."

He picked up his fork, too. "And in this moment, we're together, having a wonderful dinner, and you look beautiful, and I intend to enjoy every minute."

"Me, too."

They were still holding hands, and he rubbed his thumb over the top of hers before letting go and sitting back, preparing to eat. They nibbled on salad and sipped their wine, and then took their time with the cheese fondue, smothering cubes of baguette with the rich, gooey blend. When the next course came, Adele was already starting to feel full, so she picked at the *spätzle* and took her time savoring small bites of the tender *jaeger schnitzel*. Through it all they talked about lighter things, leaving the question of their relationship to the side.

Dan was just as entertaining as he'd always been, and she got a warm feeling deep inside when he talked about his family. He was especially close to Drew, even though they didn't see each other often with Drew traveling so much. But his stories about their antics when they were together—including the time they came face-to-face with a black bear while hiking—kept her laughing.

The evening was waning and their plates were cleared when the chocolate fondue was brought out, with a platter of fruit, cubes of banana bread and soft marshmallow.

"What about your mom, Del?" Dan changed the subject as Adele prepared to dip a strawberry in the smooth melted chocolate.

The simple question changed the mood, and Adele looked up at him as she swirled the strawberry a bit, letting the excess chocolate drip off. "I don't see her much. She's still doing her own thing. It's not that we don't get along, exactly." She took a bite of the strawberry and pondered. "It's more... we don't know each other. We never have. We call each other now and again, but it's hard to know what to talk about. I haven't seen her in three years, when I went home for a week."

"She hasn't come out here?"

Adele shook her head. "She said she doesn't like to fly. I'm not sure I believe her. I think she's just...well, in a rut. She's been this way for so long, I think she simply can't comprehend change."

"I'm really sorry. I know your relationship with her was always a bit distant."

Adele nodded and looked down at her plate. "Truth is, she wasn't around a whole lot when I was sick, either. She came right after my surgery and stayed a week, and then I was on my own again."

Dan's face darkened with anger. "I can't believe she wasn't there for you. She's your mother, for God's sake."

Adele smiled thinly. "Don't blame her too much. I told her she couldn't take a bunch of time off work and I'd be fine. Neither one of us has pushed really hard to have a relationship. I'm partly to blame."

Adele wondered if her infertility had hindered that, too. Not just because she'd never give her mom any grandchildren, but because she'd isolated herself from everyone, not just Dan. She hadn't trusted them to be there for her, so she'd bailed before they had a chance to.

She'd been reaching for a piece of marshmallow when she paused, her hand poised above the platter. She lifted her gaze and looked at Dan, so handsome in the candlelight. So…forgiving. Was he really ready to try again? After she'd hurt him so much?

She lowered her hand and looked into his eyes.

"I didn't think I'd be enough," she whispered, not trusting herself to speak any louder. "I wasn't enough to keep my dad from leaving my mom. I wasn't enough for my mom, either. I was always a…a burden. I was terrified I'd be a burden to you, too. And definitely not enough." She swallowed against a few tears that had formed, clogging her throat. "When I found out I couldn't have children… I knew it. I couldn't bear the thought of giving all of myself to you—what was left of me—and having it handed back. But I was wrong, Dan. I didn't trust you, and I should have."

His eyes were suspiciously shiny as he answered, "Yes, you should have. Because I was ready to be in it for the long haul."

They left the rest of the fondue; she was full anyway. Dan paid the check and retrieved her coat. "Do you want to walk back to the hotel?"

She had on boots and her warm coat, and it was a clear winter's night. "Let's walk to the falls. I've never seen it in the dark."

"If you want to."

She smiled. "It'll give me a chance to walk off dinner."

And the opportunity to have more time before deciding what to do.

CHAPTER THIRTEEN

ONCE OUTSIDE, SHE SLID her gloved hand into his. The night was still and silent; not even the cars on the highway were audible. The moon watched from overhead, not quite full, and the sky was full of stars. They ambled down the narrow road to the parking lot of Bow Falls, the rush of water now a dull shushing sound as they got closer. Adele's toes were a little cold, but she would warm them up later. Right now she was going to enjoy the moment.

The falls was a hulking gray arc of ice in the dark, thanks to the moonlight, while the water at the bottom was open and inky-black. "In the summer," Adele said quietly, pointing, "white water rafters leave from just there, below the falls. When the melt is on, there's a lot of water."

"I bet it sees a lot of tourists."

She smiled up at him. "The whole town does. You should be here in the summer."

And then she realized that he wouldn't be. He'd be back in Toronto, and she'd be here. Her business was here. She had clients booked for the next year. And that day-by-day thing sounded great, except for the logistics of it. As in, half a country away from each other.

How was that even possible to consider?

"You got quiet all of a sudden," Dan said. He tugged on her hand and pulled her close. They'd walked through the parking lot and closer to the stone wall near the falls. Now he guided her to a nearby tree, and they leaned against the trunk, beneath the naked branches.

"Just thinking," she replied, holding his hand tightly. It seemed like if she let go, he'd be gone forever, and she wasn't ready for that to happen yet. One more day. Just one, and a handful of hours, and he was going to Calgary. It was a fact that couldn't be ignored, even if they were trying their best.

"Thinking is highly overrated." Dan shifted so he was in front of her, his body sheltering her from the wind. Her back was against the tree trunk, and she lifted her chin the slightest bit.

"I've wanted to do this all day," he said, and then dipped his head to kiss her.

He took his time. They sipped, tasted, savored. He braced his hands against the tree and she wrapped her arms around his waist, holding him close as the kiss deepened. She didn't want to let him go. Not ever. But the time was going to come when they couldn't play vacation anymore. And when that happened, they would have to deal with the harsh reality that they'd built separate lives that couldn't just be dismissed in an instant.

"I never stopped loving you," he whispered against her hair, and she wanted to cry. She wouldn't, though. Not now. Now she was going to hold on as tightly as she could.

"Me either," she answered, breathless. "I tried. I lied to myself and said I didn't love you anymore. But I never stopped, Dan. Never."

His body pressed against hers, pinning her against the tree, and it felt glorious. "Come back with me," he urged, the words soft and persuasive. "Spend the night with me, Delly. Let me love you again."

She unwound her arms from around his

ribs and lifted a hand to touch his face. "I'll think about it. It's not a small thing you're asking. Not for us."

"No," he agreed, his eyes nearly black in the darkness. "Not for us."

He took her hand and they started the walk back to the hotel, going slowly as they climbed up the hill. She wasn't sure if she'd stay or go. She wanted to stay...wanted to very badly. Being in Dan's arms, waking with him in the morning...it was as close to heaven as she could imagine. But it scared her, too. She wouldn't walk away from this unscathed. And it could be better or a whole lot worse if they made love before he left.

When the lights of the Cascade lobby came into view, Dan pulled her off to the side, into the snow, and held her close. He kissed her until her breath was gone and her knees wobbled. "Stay," he said, his voice hoarse.

"I..." She was on the verge of saying yes, but what came out of her mouth was, "I can't."

His lips turned down in a frown.

"I want to, Dan, but I... I need time to think. This week has been such a whirlwind. A week ago you hated me. We've gone through this crazy roller coaster of confession and forgiveness and it's just..." She looked up into his face. "The last time we were on the verge of something important, I reacted with fear and on emotion and it took us apart. I don't want to do something hasty and…and jeopardize where we are."

"I'm not sure how sleeping together will jeopardize anything," he said, his gaze softening a little as his lips turned up.

It was so very tempting. "I have to be sure."

"Yes," he said quietly, "you do."

That was it then, wasn't it? For tonight, at least. She did have to be absolutely certain this was what she wanted, not just on a physical level but on all levels. She could get hurt. And the last thing she wanted to do was hurt him. "I need to go home and think. Please understand…"

"Let's get you a cab," he said softly, stepping back. "And there's nothing to understand. You have every right to say no, Del. I respect that. I can, uh, deal with my disappointment."

Her cheeks flushed, but she laughed a little. "You haven't really changed at all."

"God, I hope not." He put his arm around her shoulders and guided her back to the sidewalk. They ambled to the front entrance, and then asked the doorman for a cab. Moments later a car arrived, pulled up to the curb and idled.

Dan lifted her chin and kissed her once more, a soft, lingering type of kiss that sent tingles right to her toes. "Maybe that will help you with your thinking," he murmured, and then reached around to open the back door of the taxi.

She looked up just before he closed the door. "Thank you for a wonderful evening."

"Anytime," he answered. "What about tomorrow? Are you around so we can... I don't know, do something?"

She was a little sorry and a little relieved that she had to answer, "I'm sorry, but I've got a couple coming out to tour venues. It's been set up for weeks."

"Oh. Well, I can't monopolize all your time. Sleep well, Delly." He shut the door with a click.

The driver asked for her address and she gave it, and then sat quietly as they made the drive down the hill and into the town site. She was already thinking. And wondering if there was any way possible they could make this work.

Dan packed his bag, for real this time. Checkout was by eleven; he planned to do that and then meet Adele at her place before he had to head to Calgary. He was due in the office first thing tomorrow morning, and had a room reserved in a downtown Calgary hotel for tonight, though if things went the way he hoped, he'd be at Adele's tonight.

It didn't take long to pack; he took his things downstairs and left them with the concierge while he grabbed a quick breakfast. He was nervous as hell about what came next, though. This was the end of his week. He didn't want to leave Adele; wished he had more time so they could build a new foundation. Dread settled like a rock in the pit of his stomach. She'd said she hadn't stopped loving him, but it was a big leap from there to actually having a relationship again—especially a long-distance one.

He'd hired a car for the days ahead, and had it delivered to the hotel. With his luggage stowed securely in the trunk, he climbed behind the wheel of the Lexus and made the short trip to Adele's place, parking behind her little car in the driveway. His pulse quickened and the knot in his stomach intensified. What if she'd thought about them and decided it wasn't worth it? How was he going to get over her again?

He climbed her steps and knocked on her door, as nervous as a boy on his first date. When she opened the door, his tongue seemed to tangle in his mouth, momentarily preventing him from speaking. She wore snug jeans and a V-neck sweater made out of some sort of ultra-soft blue material, and it highlighted her curves gloriously. The other night, he'd been prevented from touching those curves by the bulkiness of her coat. Now his fingers itched to skim down her ribs and settle on her hips.

Nervousness hadn't made the wanting go away.

"Hi," she finally said, trying a smile.

"Hi."

She stepped aside, holding the door open. "Come in, please."

She sounded so...polite. That probably wasn't good. He stepped inside the warm entry and she reached for his coat. "Here, let me take this."

He let her slide it off his shoulders, but when she stood there, his coat in her hands, he knew he had to kiss her. Her eyes were wide and her lips slightly parted as he took a step closer and covered her mouth with his own.

She was so sweet. Sweet and soft and perfect, just like he remembered.

And when the kiss broke off, she put her arms around his middle and snuggled in against his chest, just for a few moments. But it eased the knot of worry and made him close his eyes, hoping.

"Did you eat?" she asked, stepping back. "I can make you something."

"I had an omelet at the hotel, but thanks."

"Eggs," she teased, and grinned up at him.

"Best way to start the day."

"So…"

"So, let's go inside and talk."

They went into the living room and sat on the sofa. Dan patted the cushion next to him. "Will you sit next to me? No matter what happens, I want to be holding your hand, all right?"

She nodded, and Dan noticed a flicker of unease behind her eyes. Still, he wasn't going to freak out yet. Even if they tried to make this work, there were a lot of things to discuss.

And as he twined his fingers with hers, he found himself wishing she'd stayed over. No matter how this went, he wished he had that final memory to take back with him.

"So," he began, hoping he came up with the

right words. "The first thing I want to say is that I want this to work out somehow. I don't want today to be goodbye forever."

She nodded. "I know. I feel the same way."

He let out a relieved breath. "Oh, thank God."

"But—"

"No, please. Don't start the next sentence with 'but.'"

She squeezed his hand. "I have to, Dan. These feelings… I need to let them out so I can deal with them. These last few days have been…transformative. Please don't doubt that I care for you so much."

"The other night, it was love."

She swallowed, nodded. "Yes. But what I'm saying is, the logistics of us being in a relationship… I don't even know how that would work. You live in Toronto. I'm in Banff."

"So that's it?" He pulled his hand away. "You're not even willing to try?"

"I didn't say that." Her voice had tensed, and he tried to quell the frustration he was feeling. He didn't want to fight. He wanted to talk this through.

"Then how do you see this working?"

"I don't know. I've gone over it a million

times in my head. We've built lives in different places. I've built this business. I have clients that I can't just abandon, and if I cancel contracts, then I have deposits and fees that have to be repaid. I can't afford to do that. It'll bankrupt me."

He understood that. It wasn't as easy as handing in a resignation and taking a new job. His father had always owned his own business and it was a very different thing.

"And," she continued, "it seems…precipitous to pack it all in on a week's reconnection. It's…it's too fast."

"You're not sure about us."

"Are you?"

He paused. Was he? If he were sure, would he have felt the stomach-twisting nerves that had plagued him all morning? Hadn't he been worried that she'd say no? He certainly hadn't trusted her to say yes.

Trust. Ah, yes. That sticky, sticky word.

"No," he whispered. "No, I'm not sure at all."

The hopeful energy in the room disappeared, replaced by something he could only describe as futility. She looked disappointed in his answer, as though she'd been waiting for him to convince her about them. Her gaze slid away from his and her shoulders rounded, just a little bit.

"It's more than closure, Delly," he tried, nudging his knee a little closer to hers. "We both know it. We're not over each other. God, the way you kissed me by the falls… the things we said…"

"I know," she replied, her voice rough. "I know. But maybe what we need to do is actually get over each other rather than beat ourselves silly trying to make something work."

"So you're not even willing to give this a chance." He knew the words came out harshly, but he didn't care. She was the only woman he'd ever truly loved. He wanted to start over. But they both had to want it. They both had to be in the same place, mentally if not geographically. Hope fizzled away, leaving him feeling so empty, it was frightening. Before he'd had his anger to keep him warm. Now he had nothing.

A loud *buzz-buzz* sounded, and his phone vibrated in his pocket.

"You should check that. It could be important."

"I don't need to. I'm not married to my phone."

Or anything or anyone else either, he thought bitterly.

An awkward silence followed, and then another loud *buzz-buzz* and a vibration.

With an annoyed sigh, he fished into his pocket for his phone and took it out and hit the button at the bottom to illuminate the screen. He scanned the text message, a smile growing on his face. At least there was some good news in his day.

"What is it?"

"It's Morgan. Tamara had a baby boy at ten thirty-seven. Three weeks early, at six pounds, three ounces."

He turned the phone around so she could see the picture of the newborn, swaddled up in flannel and a stretchy hospital cap.

"Congratulations."

Her voice was cold and anything but congratulatory. And then he knew he'd blown it. What had he been thinking? Here they were, trying to talk about their future, and he was all excited over the one thing she could never have—a baby of her own. How insensitive could he be?

"I'm sorry, Adele. I didn't think…"

"The world doesn't stop because I can't have kids, Dan."

"I know, but it was insensitive of me—"

"So what would you do, pretend all of your nieces and nephews didn't exist? Keep me away from pregnant people? Make sure there are subjects that your family wouldn't discuss in my presence? This is what I meant when I said nothing had changed."

"I didn't mean it like that. Just that the timing isn't great."

"So you walk on eggshells, is that it?"

She got up from the sofa and paced to the window overlooking the street. "Dan, you deserve someone who can blend in with your family. Who can give you what you want. I can't. I'll never be able to."

He stood up, too, suddenly angry. "I want *you*. Don't you get that? That's all I ever wanted! And you keep throwing up roadblocks!"

"Because they exist, dammit! I won't pretend they don't and then get hurt later on because I failed to face the truth. Look at my mom. My dad left before I was even born, and you know what she did? She faced up to her situation and got on with it. She provided for me all by herself. That was her reality and she sure as hell didn't pretend otherwise."

"And how has that worked for you? Reality

can be pretty damn lonely. Especially when you hide behind it so you don't have to put yourself out there and get hurt."

"How dare you judge?"

"I dare because I see it before my eyes. Why didn't your mother ever get married? I don't think you even mentioned her having any boyfriends. Why is that? Because she was scared she'd be left high and dry, like she was when your dad left her?"

Adele turned around, her eyes flashing. "You mean like you were after I left, Dan? No substantial relationships because you didn't trust anyone? Maybe you should look in the mirror before you toss judgments around."

Her accusation cut him to the quick. "Maybe I should," he admitted. "You're right. I stopped trusting."

"Do you trust me?"

He wanted to say yes. Wanted to say it and tell her that they'd figure it out and work it out and be happy, but he couldn't lie. Not anymore. Nothing but total honesty would work if they were going to look at being together again.

"No," he answered dully. "I want to. But I was scared to come over here and was afraid of what you'd say. And I'm scared that if we try to work this out, that you'll find a reason to leave me again. That…if we're apart too much, or too long, it'll make it easier for you to back out."

"Then you really don't know me at all."

"You didn't let me finish. But I'm willing to take that risk, Del. Because I don't want us to blow this a second time."

"As long as you keep me in your sights." Her eyes teared up and he wasn't sure if it was sadness or anger or both. "And this is the big problem, don't you see? You can't lock me in a box and keep me there like…like Tinkerbell so I can't get away. You have to believe in me, and you don't."

Anger flared to life. "It's not like I don't have a reason! I'm human, for God's sake. I believed in you once and you left, and that was after three years. Of course I have a problem with trust!"

Silence rang out as they faced each other, and his anger left abruptly, washed away by what felt like the pain of inevitability. What had he expected, really? That after a week and a few dates everything would be fixed?

And yet the idea that he wouldn't be with her again, wouldn't kiss her or hold her hand was like a hot knife to the gut. Because what they'd said at dinner was also true. They had never stopped loving each other.

"It doesn't mean I don't love you," he said, quieter now, emotion creating a rasp in his voice. "It doesn't mean I don't want to try. I do, Del. I want us to try. I'm trying right now."

"I know you are." Her voice broke and the tears in her eyes dropped quietly down her cheeks. "But I don't think it's enough. I can't see us making it work when we'd see each other every few months. You'd have to believe in me, Dan. Believe in us. Otherwise we're just prolonging the inevitable."

She sniffed, new tears forming at the corners of her eyes. "I know I've been clear for a long time, but there's still a part of me that wonders, every time I have a pap test, if the cancer is going to come back. Or if it will show up somewhere else."

He looked at her levelly, feeling sorry for her but also needing to give her some truths. "That could happen if we're together or not. I would have been by your side then, and I would be by your side again. Yes, I have trust issues, and I own that. But you're doing this out of fear. And I don't know what to say to combat that."

She shook her head. "I don't think there's anything you can say. The times we spent together... I had hope, you know? It felt so good. So...right. But it's not reasonable. It's not reality."

It finally clicked in his brain that from the moment she'd been born, through her cancer treatment and up until this moment, she'd been programmed to deal with "reality."

"Reality is overrated," he replied.

She made a sound of frustration, and he smiled a little.

"Tell me, Delly, if you're so into reality, why wedding planning? Seems to me that it's one day that is really overblown and a fantasy. Not really a representation of the reality of marriage."

"Because that will come soon enough. Commitments take work. Dedication. Even when it's rough. And at least I can help couples get off to a memorable start."

"Huh." It seemed she knew well enough what made a strong relationship. She just wasn't willing to put in the work with them.

This was it, then. No coming up with workable solutions or plans, no confessions of love and a willingness to try anything to see it through. Instead, this was ending the way he'd expected at the beginning of the week, with a few pleasurable interludes in between. This was goodbye.

"Dan, I'm sorry. I turned this around in my head and—"

He held up his hand. "No, it's okay. I was just kidding myself, hoping again. You're right. We spent a few days together, ignoring the 'reality' of the situation. I'll go now, Del. No hard feelings."

His feelings were hard, indeed, but he didn't want to leave this with nothing but anger between them. If this was really the end, he wanted them to have a goodbye.

"I'm... I'm sorry," she said, her voice breaking.

"Me too."

He went to the entry and reached for his jacket. Shrugged it on and turned toward the door, watched as Adele stood there helplessly. He had his hand on the doorknob when he turned around again, cradled her face in his hands and put one final kiss on her lips. They trembled beneath his...or perhaps that was his own. A man shouldn't have to say goodbye to the woman he loved twice in his life.

Before she could say anything, he turned

and went out the door, down the stairs, back to his car. Started it as if on autopilot, backed out of the driveway, made his way to the highway and east toward Calgary.

Maybe she was right. Maybe it was time to live in reality again. And he'd been right, too. Reality sucked.

CHAPTER FOURTEEN

ADELE STOOD IN her entry for what seemed like an hour, but was probably only a minute or two. Certainly long enough for Dan to get in his car and drive away. For good. Long enough for the silence to confirm that he wasn't coming back. And that she'd pushed him away again.

And while she wasn't sure what else she could have done, she couldn't escape the feeling that it was so utterly, utterly wrong.

Quiet footsteps took her back to the living room, where she sank down onto the sofa, staring straight ahead. Numb. She wasn't really feeling anything at all until Mr. Num-Nums jumped up on the sofa with a soft chirp and climbed onto her lap, all warm and soft and reassuring.

She started to cry. To cry like she hadn't in years. Not since the day she'd found out she'd need a hysterectomy. Since she'd broken up with Dan the first time, when she'd been so sure she was sending him off to better things and she was dealing with her own crisis. This was different.

Worse. Somehow, this was worse.

She cried into Mr. Num-Nums's fur and he let her, as if he knew she needed him to stay. After a long time, she sobbed her way to the kitchen and poured a glass of wine, her hand shaking. She sat in the dark and drank it, trying to staunch her tears and get a grip on herself. But nothing chased away the empty hole in the pit of her stomach, the awful burn of knowing he was gone.

At seven o'clock she broke down and called Harper, because she simply didn't want to be alone anymore.

Harper showed up with emergency wine, chocolate, potato chips and a box of tissues. Arms full, she enveloped Adele in a warm hug, the bags of stuff clunking against Adele's back. "I'm so sorry, honey."

"Oh, Harper."

"Come on. Let's go in and you can tell me everything."

Harper took over, pouring more wine, putting chips in a bowl and opening the little box of chocolate truffles. Adele sat on the sofa again, feeling slightly cheered as Harper handed her a glass of wine and a piece of chocolate. "Seriously. Put that in your mouth and let it melt. It's my Callebaut emergency stash."

"The fact that you have an emergency stash at all and can stay out of it is testament to your willpower."

"Don't be silly. I lock it up at the studio. I have to really want it to go over there and fetch it."

Adele laughed, something she hadn't expected to do. She ate the truffle—divine—and sipped the wine. Closed her eyes and let out a big breath.

"Okay," Harper said firmly. "Now you can tell me what happened that made your face look like crap."

"Dan's gone."

"I gathered that." She leaned back and sipped from her glass. "What happened?"

"What didn't?" Now that Adele had had a good cry, she could speak without losing it. "I haven't talked to you in a few days. We went dogsledding…it was so fun…and then a real dinner date. Our feelings…" Her throat clogged again and she took a moment, plus another good pull of wine before continuing. "We admitted we hadn't stopped loving each other. And he wanted me to stay with him all night, but I didn't. I had to think."

"Uh-oh." Harper reached into the chip bowl. "I know what that means."

"What?"

She crunched down on a chip. "Oh, honey. You overthink things. You think them to death. It works great in your business, but in life…sometimes you have to go with your gut. Fly by the seat of your pants."

"I don't overthink. I just deal with what's in front of me."

"Sure. Okay, go on. Then what happened?"

"Then he came here today and…" She paused, but when she spoke again, it all came out in a rush. "And he wanted to try again, but he doesn't trust me not to hurt him again. And then his sister had a baby and I still can't give him the family he wants and how could we make it work between Toronto and here? It doesn't make sense. And so he left."

Harper stared at her. "I hope you weren't that blunt."

"It's not that I don't love him. I do."

"Then what the hell is the problem?" Harper put her glass down on the table and sat back, folding her hands in her lap. "Listen, Adele, I love you. You're the closest thing to a sister I've ever had. But you don't let yourself get close to anyone, including me. I've known all along that you were guarding secrets. How can you really love someone if you don't let them in? And that's what you did to Dan, all those years ago. You deprived him of the joy—and yes, the pain—of being by your side when you were sick. You spoke for him and took his voice. Would you want someone to do that to you?"

Adele's mouth dropped open.

"I know, this is some serious tough love, but you can't go on this way. You're a wedding planner. Why does everyone get a happy-ever-after but you? Don't you think you deserve it?"

Her throat started to burn.

"And of course Dan doesn't trust you yet. You broke his heart. You left. It's natural he'd be afraid you might do it again, and it's up to you to prove otherwise. But by God, you need to fight for him if you want him."

Harper let out a big breath, reached for her wine and took a gulp.

"If you'd seen his face when he got the text about his new nephew," Adele whispered.

"And you can't have kids. This is not a new development, and you told Dan, and he still fell for you again this week. I mean, has he actually come out and said it would be a deal breaker?"

"Of course not, but—"

"No buts. Sweetie, this is you putting up walls. I don't know why, but I recognize it when I see it." She tempered her voice and touched Adele's knee. "I'm not saying it wasn't devastating. I can see that it was. And I'm not trying to be insensitive, but I have to ask. Does your infertility make you feel like less of a woman?"

Adele thought about it for a minute, still reeling from the blunt but caring speech she'd been treated to. "No. I'm not less of a woman. A woman isn't defined by her reproductive parts. But somehow, I feel like…a mother is."

Harper's gaze softened. "I'm going to tell you a little something about myself that I don't usually tell. I'm adopted. I was adopted at birth by my mom and dad and I can tell you right now, that motherhood isn't defined by reproductive parts, either. Because that's biology, and motherhood…" She leaned over and put her hand on Adele's heart. "That's in here. If you open it up and take a chance."

Adele sniffed again, swiped at her eyes with her right hand and took the hand Harper had over her heart in her left. "Why didn't I call you yesterday?" she wailed.

Harper sighed. "Because you're scared. And in love. And you're letting logistics get conveniently in the way. If you truly want a solution, you'll find a solution. I promise. Now let's finish this chocolate, binge on the chips, drink the wine and have a sleepover. We can talk until the wee hours and then tomorrow you can decide what you're going to do."

Adele blinked away the moisture in her lashes and smiled. "You are a great friend, Harper."

"I know. Now, pass the chips."

Dan sat at a makeshift desk in the downtown office and tapped his pen against the legal pad in front of him. He usually used a pen and paper to jot down notes—there was still something about working things out in ink that he liked—but today he'd hardly done anything but doodle on the top page.

Oh, he'd worked on his laptop and had a call with head office as a follow-up to a report he'd received, but he couldn't stop thoughts of Adele from sneaking in every moment he wasn't busy.

This morning he'd sat in on a meeting with the office staff and he'd been duly impressed with their positive, proactive attitude and teamwork to get things up and running as quickly and smoothly as possible. They were dealing with new contracts and site construction while still working out the kinks of setting up a new office. It had been exciting, actually. More than he'd expected. Back in Toronto, he'd seen all this information on paper and in columns of black and red. Seeing it in motion was a totally different thing.

He should just enjoy it while he was here, and then head back on Thursday. He had a new nephew to see, after all.

The thought cheered him more than anything else had all week. It was difficult to get excited about going home when it felt like there was very little there waiting for him.

Steve, the branch manager, stepped into Dan's temporary office and shut the door. "Hey, I wanted to get your thoughts on something."

"Sure. Fire away." Dan was happy to have another distraction. Eventually he wouldn't need them, right? It would just take time.

Steve sat and Dan thought he looked a little nervous, the way he was perched on his chair instead of relaxing against the back. He wasn't smiling, either. Dan put down his pen. "What's up, Steve? You don't look happy."

"I know you're not in HR or anything, but I need some advice. Or just a sounding board… I don't know. The thing is, the office is just getting off the ground, and…"

Dan leaned forward. "Just spell it out." He smiled a little. "It can't be that bad." Were there staffing issues? Supplier or jobsite complications?

"My wife's had an opportunity come her way and I want her to take it. It's unlikely another chance like this will come again, especially at our age. It seems like anything over fifty and suddenly you're seen as having a short shelf life."

Dan nodded. "Instead of realizing that your years of experience bring a depth to the management table. I understand."

Steve nodded. "I know you're young, but I'm glad you get it. The thing is, the job's in London."

Dan sat back. "England?"

Steve nodded. "At a hospital there. The kids are mostly grown, and…" Steve grinned at this point, his eyes lighting up. "Seriously, it feels like a new beginning for us. Exciting and we're nowhere near as broke as we were when we were newlyweds with secondhand furniture and twenty bucks left on payday."

Dan nodded. "So...you'd go to London with her."

Steve nodded. "Yeah. Not until March, so it's not like it's next week or anything, but yeah. That would be the plan. But I don't want to screw over the company, either. I've put in a lot of years and I care about what happens. It's a crucial time, and managing the office here...well, I did and still do appreciate the confidence the company's placed in me."

Dan looked at the older man, hair graying at his temples, but his blue eyes alight with the idea of a new adventure. There was no question in Dan's mind what he should do. "Of course you should go. You wouldn't want her to miss out on this, and I'm guessing that you don't want to do this apart, either."

"She's worked hard and supported me all this time. It's her turn, you know? And being apart...well, we've been together for twenty-five years. That's just a nonstarter." He smiled. "We'd be miserable. It's a sacrifice I'm happy to make. It's just hard because

I feel as if you placed your trust in me and I'm bailing."

"You're not bailing. You're choosing a life over a job. No one doubts your dedication—you know that. We'll work it out."

Steve rose from his chair and held out his hand. "You know, one of the things I've always loved about this company is that the people seem to come first. I'm going to miss that."

Dan shook his hand with a firm grip. "Talk to HR and put in your resignation, and I'll have a word with Brian, too." The CEO would likely have someone in mind to take over, anyway. "It'll all work out. I'm happy for you."

"Thanks. I'm heading out for the day, but I'll see you tomorrow?"

"Yeah. I have another day before jetting back to the real world."

"Too bad. It's been nice having you around. Your ideas in the meeting this morning were great."

"Hey, I'm more than just a pretty face. Or a bean counter," Dan quipped. "Take it easy, Steve."

"You too. And thanks for the ear."

After Steve was gone, Dan sat back in his

chair and thought about what had just happened. Steve had risen through the ranks of the company after he'd left his job in aviation and had gone to work as a service tech for wind turbines. He'd earned this position from years of dedication and initiative. But he was willing to put it all to the side to support his wife in a new opportunity. Some would call him foolish, but Dan respected him even more than he had before.

His thoughts turned to Adele. Did they have this sort of relationship? Could they have? Was he willing to sacrifice his dream for hers?

He picked up his pen and started doodling again, just a series of squiggles on the yellow pad. He thought back to when she'd broken up with him. She'd left so he could follow his dream of a great career and big family. She'd been the one to sacrifice, even if it had been utterly misguided. And while he was still angry that she'd taken the choice away from him—surely that wasn't a sign of a great relationship—he now understood that she'd sacrificed her own happiness for what she thought would be his. As she'd said once: wrong thing for the right reasons.

She'd sacrificed once…so why should he demand she do so again?

He turned the thoughts over and over in his brain as he checked his watch and made a call through to Toronto, informing Brian of the impending situation. Thought of it while he stayed in the office far too late, not looking forward to returning to the hotel and eating alone again. He ordered in instead, and picked at the Vietnamese noodles listlessly. What he wanted to do was jump in his car and drive to Banff and knock on her door. But he wasn't sure what he'd say. She'd been very definite, hadn't she?

In the end, he finally went back to the hotel to try to get some sleep.

At eight in the morning, he was back at the office. He walked in the door and saw the receptionist already at her desk. "Good morning, Kirsten," he greeted, smiling.

"Good morning, Dan. There're already a few messages in your office for you."

"Thanks. When Steve comes in, can you let him know I want to meet with him when he gets a moment?"

"Certainly."

He offered greetings to the other staff already there, went to the kitchen to make a fresh coffee and caught up with a few of the engineers. The entire vibe was one of energy and collaboration, and he realized that Steve had done a great job of staffing. A mix of new, innovative talent and experience gave a very balanced feel to the office, and everyone seemed enthusiastic and ready to do their jobs.

It wasn't quite like this at corporate. Oh, it was nice enough, and friendly, but it was also more formal. More about numbers and graphs and contracts, and less about building and collaborating.

He'd made his way up through the finance department in record time, but he got the feeling that was due to long hours and not actual love of the work.

Which got him thinking all over again.

By three o'clock, he had doodled on four different pages of his legal pad and couldn't quite believe what he was thinking. And maybe corporate wouldn't even go for it. He was the youngest C-suite executive the company had ever had, and he was actually considering taking a demotion. But deep in his gut, he was excited by the idea of a challenge. And he would be within an hour of Adele. If logistics and distance were part of the bigger issue, this would eliminate at least one barrier. Because the one thing he was sure of was that he still loved her. He was angry with her, yes. And he had his own issues to work on. But loving her had never been a question.

He spoke with Steve once more, and after the other man left, Dan found himself asking himself one other important question. If it didn't work out with Adele, would he still want to be here? Or would he be perfectly happy in his old life?

The answer came to him so quickly, he knew it had to be true. She'd been right about something else, too. He'd filled his life with his path to success because it was all he had. Now he wanted more. He couldn't keep running away.

He had to see her. But first he had to talk to Brian and float an idea past him.

When he hung up the phone an hour later, he sat back in his chair and rubbed his hand over his face. It would have to go through the proper channels, of course, before anything was finalized. But Brian had taken his idea and expanded on it in a way that was unexpected.

He'd packed up for the day when the phone

on his desk beeped. "Dan, there's someone here to see you. A Miss Hawthorne."

His heart gave a solid thump. She was here? "I'll be right out. Thanks, Kirsten."

She was here.

She'd come to find him.

And then the next thought: he couldn't blow this. Not again.

He stood, straightened his tie, checked his shirttails and ran his hand over his hair. Then, taking a big breath, he stepped out of the office and into the reception area.

CHAPTER FIFTEEN

ADELE WAS SURE her knees were knocking under her long skirt.

She was so nervous, she was nauseated. And she'd spent fifteen minutes in her cold car, redoing her makeup and going over what she wanted to say. Naturally, now that she was inside Dan's company's office, the words had flown out of her brain.

The receptionist was sweet as pie and had called Dan. Adele couldn't think about sitting in one of the reception chairs, so she stood, knees weak, breath short, unsure of how this could work, but knowing she had to try. Harper had been right. It was time for her to fight for the life she wanted and stop running from it.

He turned the corner. Stopped. Met her eyes, and her lip started trembling.

And then he was striding toward her, big,

purposeful steps, and she was lunging forward, too, until he caught her in a bear hug and held her tight.

Her first feeling was that of relief. Then hope. And then…coming home.

The receptionist discreetly cleared her throat.

Dan pressed a kiss to her hair and stepped back, his face pink as he turned to the woman behind the desk. "Sorry about that, Kirsten. Long story."

She merely smiled warmly. "And one with a happy ending, it looks like. I just thought you might like to, uh, speak in your office."

A quick glance showed at least four pairs of eyes watching while trying to appear as if they weren't.

"Good idea." Dan took Adele's hand, and had only tugged her a step when he stopped again. "Adele, this is Kirsten. Kirsten, Adele."

"Nice to meet you," Adele stammered, heat rising in her cheeks.

"Likewise. And I love your boots."

Adele laughed, a sound that was more incredulous than anything, and choked out a "thank you" as Dan tugged her hand again and led her to a small office on the left and shut the door behind him.

He dropped her hand and met her gaze, and all her fears rushed back and the words she searched for dashed away again.

"You came," he said quietly.

"I had to see you. To tell you…" To tell him what? *Everything*, her brain answered, but she had to put those thoughts into complete sentences.

He just waited. She could hear her heartbeat in her ears. Dan touched her forearm and said, "You look beautiful today."

Beautiful. Right. She took a shaky breath. "I dressed up." Because today was important, and on important days, a person dressed for the occasion.

"Do you want me to take your coat?" He hesitated a beat, and then asked earnestly, "Are you staying long enough for that?"

She nodded briefly, and started undoing buttons. The panels fell open and she unwound the scarf around her neck. "Thank you."

"No problem." He helped her take it off and draped it over a nearby credenza. "I'm so glad you're here."

"You are?" Oh, that was a good sign, right?

"I am. In case my hug out there left you with any doubts." And a smile ticked up one corner of his mouth, and she relaxed a few degrees.

"Harper told me I was an idiot. And that I should fight for you." No preamble. Just flat-out truth. She didn't know how else to do this.

His eyes widened. "I see."

He wasn't going to make this easy for her, but maybe it shouldn't be. Maybe it was time to really let him see everything. She wasn't good at making herself vulnerable, and she really wasn't good at leaving things to chance. But if the alternative was losing him forever, again, she knew she had to do something differently.

"Dan?"

"What, Delly?"

"I'm an idiot, and I've come here to fight for you, and to tell you that I'll do what it takes to make this work. I don't have the answers, and I'm scared to death, but I'm here."

Her insides trembled, but Dan put a reassuring hand along the side of her face and smiled at her tenderly. "Oh, sweetheart," he said softly, "I was about to drive to Banff and tell you exactly the same thing."

Relief slammed into her. "You were?"

He nodded, his eyes warm on hers. "Yes. The first time, I let you walk away, and this time, I did the walking. But now I want to fight for us. I love you, Delly. I love you so much, I haven't been able to think straight ever since I arrived at the Cascade and you walked into the lobby with Holly."

She moved into his arms again, this time the hug less fevered and more measured and with a sense of comfort and rightness that had been missing for eight long years.

"Oh, thank God. I love you, too," she whispered, breathing in his scent, memorizing the feel of him, all broad shoulders and chest and strong arms as he held her close. "I was so scared you were done with us. We wasted so much time."

He shook his head. "No, we didn't. And you know why? Because I think this is exactly where we're supposed to be. Maybe we wouldn't have made it if we'd tried when we were younger. All I know is we're here now. And we're going to figure this out."

Adele finally stepped back. "I have so many things I need to say. Things I need to ask."

"Then why don't we sit down? Or do you want to go somewhere else?"

She shook her head. What she wanted to say needed to be said now, before she lost her nerve. "This is fine. I mean…it doesn't matter where I am, as long as we're together and talking, you know?"

He pulled two chairs over and they sat knee-to-knee.

"Is not having kids a deal breaker for you?"

"No."

She was surprised at his immediate and blunt answer. "But, Dan, I know you always wanted children."

"Yes, but it's not a deal breaker. Because I love you, Del. And because, if we don't have children, it'll be fine. I've thought about it since you told me, and if we do decide we want to, we can look at options. But please, realize that you're not denying me anything."

Her pulse quickened. He'd said "if we don't have children" and "if we do decide to," which meant he was talking about the future. Their future.

"And the trust thing... Dan, I never wanted to leave you. I know it's hard for you to trust I won't leave again, but I'll do everything I can to show you I'm in it for good. It'll take time and...and..."

She paused, because this was the hard part, the bit she'd struggled over for the last few days. "And if it makes things easier, I can move the business. I can try to move my clients to someone new so they don't lose any of their bookings, and reopen somewhere else to protect my credit rating. I hate to put it in such cold business terms, but I love what I do. I can do it somewhere else, but I don't want to give it up."

Dan shook his head, squeezing her hand. "No, it's not cold at all. It's responsible, and I wouldn't want you to give it up. I love that you aren't just thinking about yourself but want to take care of your clients. Which brings me to something I want to say, Del."

"Oh."

He twined his fingers with hers. "I don't want you to move the business. The truth is, I've realized that my success was built on a habit of avoidance. I worked long hours, climbed the ladder, but inside, in here…" He pointed to his chest. "In here, I was empty. From the outside, it looked like I had it all. But I didn't. Not even close. I had this great position and I didn't have you, and one couldn't make up for the other. I don't want you to move. I want to make a change. I've been thinking about it all day, and I just got off the phone with the board of directors. Our branch manager here just resigned. They need someone to take over the Calgary operations and I want to be the one to do it."

Her head swam with what he'd just said.

He'd be living only an hour away if he took this job. And she wasn't naive; she knew that going from CFO to a branch management position was a step backward. He was willing to do that for her? Hope soared in her chest.

"You're sure you don't want to look for something bigger, here? There's got to be a lot of opportunity. You shouldn't throw away all you've accomplished, Dan. We can work something out, I promise."

But he shook his head. "I have loved being in this office, and being a part of building something new, and seeing the teamwork in place. It's exciting. And it's not like there won't be future growth. The market for clean energy sources is only going to go up with new innovations. I can be a part of that in real time, not just from a high-rise in Toronto. It's not a demotion, Del. More of a lateral move. I'd be VP of Western Operations. I'd oversee this office, as well as Edmonton, the one opening in BC and any future branches."

"You really want to do this."

"I do. And it means you can stay where you are, and we can be together, and I can love you all the time."

Her lip wobbled again. "I'm sorry I kept

244 BEST MAN FOR THE WEDDING PLANNER

pushing you away. I was so scared. You were right about the reality thing. I've always been so afraid to hope. To…dream. The closest I ever got was putting together all these weddings for strangers, you know? But Harper made me see that I deserve a happy ending, too. And maybe it won't be perfect, but we'll be together, and that's all that matters."

"Come here," he said, and pulled on her fingers. "Sit on my lap. I need you closer."

She did as he asked, even though the chair was awkward. Still, he wrapped his arms around her and put his forehead on her shoulder. "God, I'm so glad you're here. That you changed your mind."

"Me too," she whispered, closing her eyes. "I love you, Dan. And I'm so tired of letting fear hold me back."

"Then let's not," he said, leaning back and looking up into her face. "Let's do it up right and stop wasting time. Marry me, Delly. I can tie up loose ends at home and come back. You can plan our wedding instead of someone else's, and I can commute for a while until we decide if we want to live somewhere else."

"Maybe Canmore," she said, feeling a spark of excitement. "Or Springbank. Somewhere we can both travel easily…"

"Whatever. I don't care, as long as you're there."

"Me either."

"Is that a yes? Will you marry me? Finally?"

She'd been a planner all her life. She'd played the cards she was dealt, rather than taking a gamble. But it had all led to this moment, a make-or-break moment, and there was no way she was going to let it slip through her fingers again.

"That's a yes."

He stood up so fast that he nearly dumped her off his lap, but caught her again and pulled her in for a jubilant kiss.

"I love you. I'm gonna say it until you get sick of it, you hear me?"

Adele closed her eyes and held him close. Walking away from him had been her biggest mistake, and she was blessed to have a second chance.

"I'm never gonna get sick of it," she said, and he picked her up and swung her around while she laughed from sheer joy.

CHAPTER SIXTEEN

THE VOWS HAD been said, the champagne drunk and the cake cut. While it wasn't as grand a wedding as most, Adele looked out from the balcony of the Fiori Cascade and sighed a happy sigh. A chinook had formed, and the west wind had made the late March day unseasonably warm, with a scent of spring in the air. The mountains still held their cap of white and would for another month or two. All in all, it had been a magical day, and one of the fastest weddings she'd ever put together.

"What are you thinking, Mrs. Brimicombe?" Dan came up beside her and put his hand on her waist.

"I'm thinking that I'm the luckiest woman in the world."

"Funny." He gave her waist a squeeze. "I was thinking the same thing."

"That you're the luckiest woman in the world? Interesting."

He laughed, and she delighted in the sound. There was nothing she enjoyed more than teasing him.

"It's been a good day."

"Yes," she said, "it has."

Dan's entire family had flown out for the wedding, and so had Adele's mother, to Adele's great surprise. They'd had a small ceremony with family and a few friends, including Harper, who'd passed her photo duties on to another photographer and instead stood as Adele's maid of honor.

They hadn't wanted anything elaborate, though the setting was gorgeous enough. The people that meant the most to them, some champagne and a full-on high tea for the guests, ending with wedding cake with Adele's favorite buttercream filling. Tonight they'd stay in the honeymoon suite. Tomorrow they'd fly first to Vancouver, and then to Hawaii for a short but lovely six-day honeymoon.

Everyone was still mingling, and the jazz band they'd hired remained in the salon. Harper stepped out on the balcony, stunning in a dress of pale blue silk. "I thought I might find you two out here."

"And so we are."

"I missed taking your pictures today. But I'm more honored to stand with you."

Adele gave her a hug. "Thank you. If it weren't for your tough love, I doubt we'd be standing here. I wouldn't have wanted anyone else."

"And Drew can't take his eyes off you," Dan added, grinning at her. His brother was best man, and he hadn't seemed at all upset at being paired with Harper for the trip down the aisle.

Harper laughed. "Your brother is a charmer and a flirt. I see right through him. Anyway, I'm glad I caught you out here, because I want to give you your wedding present."

She reached into her jeweled clutch purse and took out a blue envelope.

"Harper, you didn't need to do this. You've done so much already."

There was something in Harper's eyes that told Adele that this was no ordinary gift, though, and so she reached for the card and opened it.

Inside was a card with a pen-and-ink sketch on the front. Adele wrinkled her brow in confusion. The sketch was of a woman who resembled Adele, and a man—Dan, of course. But in Adele's arms was a bundle that looked oddly like a baby.

She lifted confused eyes to her friend.

"This is an offer from me to you, and you're under no obligation to accept, of course. I want to help you have a baby."

Adele reached for Dan's hand. "I need to sit down."

They made their way to a wood-and-iron bench and sat, Dan holding Adele's hand while Harper sat on her other side.

"I don't understand," Dan said.

"It's like this. I love Adele, and she loves you, and I know the two of you would make wonderful parents. And so I'm offering to help you...by being your surrogate."

Adele's heart nearly stopped. "But Harper. That's... Do people really do that?"

"Sometimes." Harper smiled softly. "I'm healthy, Adele. And I'm seriously not using my uterus right now or for the foreseeable future. I'd like to do this for you both."

"I don't know what to say." Indeed, she didn't. This was a huge thing Harper was offering. So huge, she wasn't sure she could even consider it. "It's nine months of... Oh, Harper."

Tears stung the backs of her eyes. Her feelings were so overwhelming. Incredulity, hope, joy, fear.

Harper put a hand on Adele's back and rubbed gently. "If it's me, you can be involved every step of the way. You can go to doctor appointments with me, and hear the heartbeat, and feel the baby kick, and you can go to childbirth classes and be my coach. You wouldn't get to do those things if you had a different surrogate, or if you adopted. It's the one thing that you want most in the world, Adele. Let me help you."

Adele looked over at Dan. He was trying valiantly not to cry and not succeeding very well.

"I don't know what to say," he murmured, his voice catching. "This is so unexpected. So selfless, Harper. God..."

Adele pulled herself together. "We need to think about it, and talk about what it would mean for us. But, Harper, you are the best of friends. My sister from another mister. That you offered means so much."

They hugged and Harper cleared her throat a little as emotion overwhelmed. "Listen, you don't want to go in there with puffy faces and red eyes. Your photographer can only retouch so much."

They laughed and the mood lightened as they rose from the bench. Adele reached over and gave Harper's hand a squeeze. "We'll talk it over. Promise."

Harper nodded. "And we can do some research together, if you like. Okay?"

Adele nodded, and Harper slipped away, leaving her alone with Dan.

"That... Adele. Your friend is one in a million."

"I never imagined she'd offer something like that. I mean, once you and I were together, I told her a lot about what it had been like. My illness, and my feelings about not having kids. But I never expected she'd offer to carry a child for us."

Dan pulled her into a hug and kissed her hair, and then set her back again and met her gaze once more. "Just so you know, Mrs. Brimicombe, if this doesn't happen, it's okay. We have each other and that's enough. I love you. My dreams already came true today."

"Oh, Dan." Her smile wobbled. "Mine, too."

"But..."

"But…"

With possibilities echoing in their minds, they entered the ballroom together, to start their life as a family.

* * * * *

Look out for the next story in the Marrying a Millionaire duet

Coming soon!

And if you enjoyed this story, check out these other great reads from Donna Alward

The Cowboy's Convenient Bride
The Cowboy's Christmas Family
The Cowboy's Homecoming
Hired: The Italian's Bride

All available now!